Kate's fingers touched the slips of paper. She stirred them around, waiting to see if any of them called to her. Finally she just grabbed one and took it out. She unfolded it and looked at what was written there. "Santeria," she said.

"A very interesting one," remarked Sophia.

"I've never heard of it," Kate said.

"Don't worry," Sophia reassured her. "We'll point you in the right direction."

Kate went back to her friends. As the rest of the class went up and selected their slips, they talked about their choices.

"Checking out these different pagan religions sounded fun at first," Cooper said. "Now I'm not so sure."

"I certainly didn't think I'd be seeing Freya again this soon," remarked Annie.

"I don't even know what mine is," Kate said. "At least you guys have a clue."

"I guess we'll all find out soon enough what's in store for us," Cooper told her friends. "Whatever it is, it's sure to be interesting."

"Famous last words," Kate said.

Follow the Circle:

circle of three

BOOK
10

making the saint

isobel bird

AVON BOOKS

An Imprint of HarperCollinsPublishers

Library of Congress Catalog Card Number: 2001116351

ISBN 0-06-447367-8

First Avon edition, 2001

❖

AVON TRADEMARK REG. U.S. PAT. OFF. AND IN OTHER COUNTRIES,
MARCA REGISTRADA, HECHO EN U.S.A.

Visit us on the World Wide Web!
www.harperteen.com

CHAPTER 1

"Ready to kick some butt?" Cooper asked Jane.

They were standing in the backstage area of Bar None. Peering through the curtains, the girls could see a crowd gathered around the small stage, listening to the band that was playing. Some people were nodding their heads along with the driving bass line being hammered out by the band's lead singer, whose throaty voice matched the forceful music he was playing. Listening to him, Cooper had to admit that he was good—really good.

Unfortunately, the singer was her boyfriend, T.J., and the band was Schroedinger's Cat, which she and T.J. had founded together. She had quit three weeks before, when they'd told her that they thought her music was getting "too witchy." This was the first time Cooper had heard them play without her. While the split with the band had been friendly, if undeniably difficult, Cooper found herself feeling a little bit jealous that they'd been able to carry on without her guitar playing and singing.

"Don't let them get to you," Jane told her, noting her friend's expression.

Cooper smiled at her new songwriting partner. She'd met Jane shortly after leaving the band. Jane had been playing the guitar and singing on a street corner. Attracted by her lyrics and her skillful playing, Cooper had struck up a conversation with her. She and Jane had become friends, and lately they'd been playing together a lot. Both of them had been hesitant to start writing with someone else, but they'd created a couple of songs they were happy with. So when Cooper had seen Bar None's Battle of the Bands flyer, she'd suggested to Jane that they try their stuff out in front of a live audience.

At first Jane had said no. But Cooper had worked on her, and finally Jane had given in and said she would do it. Cooper suspected that Jane had agreed simply to get her to shut up, but that was fine with her. The important thing was that they were about to perform in front of a live audience. Standing there, waiting to go on, she felt the familiar mix of anticipation and nervousness coursing through her veins.

Schroedinger's Cat finished their number and the band members walked backstage. T.J. came over to Cooper and stopped, wiping the sweat from his forehead. "What did you think?" he asked, grinning.

Cooper snorted. "You call that music?" she said, taunting him. "I've heard better songs on an 'N SYNC album."

T.J. laughed. "Good thing the audience gets the last word, then," he said. "We'll see who they pick." He nodded toward the main room, where the sound of the cheering audience was still deafening. "Listen to that. I think it's safe to say we have it in the bag."

"What do *they* know?" Jane said caustically. "They're probably the same ones who made Celine Dion a star."

"T.J., meet Jane," Cooper said.

T.J. reached out and shook Jane's hand. "So you're the one who stole my girlfriend away from me," he said jokingly.

"Hey," Jane said. "Don't blame me if you're a lousy kisser."

"Now I see why you two get along so well," remarked T.J. to Cooper.

"Wait until you hear us sing," replied his girlfriend.

Just then the emcee of the evening walked to the microphone and said, "That was Schroedinger's Cat, people. I have no idea what the name means, but they were pretty rocking, don't you think?"

The audience clapped and cheered. Then the emcee continued. "Now we've got another great act for you," he said. "Cooper and Jane, otherwise known as the Bitter Pills."

"The Bitter Pills?" T.J. repeated, giving Cooper a look. "How appropriate."

"Yeah, well, we'll see how easily you guys can swallow us down when we win this thing," Cooper said. She gave him a quick kiss and then followed Jane as she walked onstage.

The two of them plugged their guitars into the amps that were set up beside the microphones. Cooper looked at Jane. "Here goes nothing," she said, and launched into the song they'd chosen to perform for the contest, "Danger Girl."

"Don't tell me what to do," she sang, the words hard and fierce. "Don't tell me what to say."

Her fingers moved across the strings of her guitar, coaxing the melody out. Beside her, Jane was playing as well. Her eyes were closed as she unleashed the fierce rhythms of the song, and her long dark hair hung in her face.

"I'm not your little baby. I'm not your sweetest thing," Cooper sang, pouring herself into the lyrics. She was swept up in the music, and she felt powerful. She could do anything. She could say anything. And no one could stop her. She had become the girl in their song.

When she reached the chorus, Jane joined her, her throaty voice blending perfectly with Cooper's. "I'm the one they said would steal your heart," they purred. "I'm the one they said would steal your soul. I'm the one they said would turn the world upside down. I'm a danger girl."

After another verse, Jane launched into a guitar solo. Cooper stood back and let her friend take center stage. Jane unleashed a torrent of notes, and Cooper looked out at the audience to see how they were responding to what they heard. She saw a lot of astonished faces, and she knew that she and Jane had surprised some people. *Why does it always shock them that girls can rock?* she thought as the solo came to an end.

The crowd was really into the song. Many of them—particularly the girls—were waving their fists in the air. Some even sang along on the chorus, their voices joining Cooper's and Jane's as they learned the words. On the last line, Cooper really let loose, her voice rising to a wail as she sang the last words. She let the final notes hang in the air as Jane finished with a flurry of licks on her guitar. Then the two of them stood side by side as the club erupted in applause. Whistling and clapping filled the air, and people called out their approval.

"I think they liked it," Cooper said to Jane.

They left the stage, slipping behind the curtain as the crowd continued to cheer. Cooper saw T.J. and the other members of Schroedinger's Cat standing there, looking at her. T.J. had a big grin on his face.

"What did you think?" Cooper asked him, putting her guitar down.

T.J. nodded his head. "Not bad," he said. "It needs some polishing, but it's a good start. I'd be happy to help you out if you want."

"Give me a break," said Jane. "We made you guys look like Britney Spears's backup band."

They all laughed. Then their attention turned to

the emcee, who had once more taken the stage and was talking to the audience.

"What did you all think of the Bitter Pills?" he asked.

The crowd let loose again, clapping madly. When they quieted down the emcee continued. "Well, we're not done yet," he said. "We've got one more act to hear tonight before we declare a winner. So let's find out what this next performer has for us. Give it up for Voodoo Mama."

As the emcee left the stage the lights switched from blue to red, and a mirrored ball somewhere above them began to turn, scattering flashes of red over the walls and ceiling. The effect was disorienting, as the shadows that flickered over everything made it seem as if faces and objects were moving rapidly from place to place when really they were standing still.

Then the sound of a single guitar floated out of the darkness. The notes came slowly and fluidly, like honey dripping from a spoon. Cooper felt a chill creep along her skin, and she shuddered as the music reached out and took hold of her. It was enticing and disturbing at the same time, a mixture of blues and something else she couldn't quite identify.

The guitar played for a minute, the player still hidden in the shadows so that the sound seemed to be coming from nowhere. Then a figure stepped forward and walked silently to the microphone. It was a girl. A single pale spotlight lit her as she reached up and cupped her hands around the mike. She was wearing a simple red dress, and her hair was done in numerous long twisting braids that fell around her shoulders.

"Midnight," she sang, the single word pouring out of her mouth in a low growl that seemed to swell and fill the room. "And you call my name."

The girl barely moved as she sang, her body swaying slightly. Accompanied only by the invisible guitarist, she let her voice convey the emotion behind her words. Her song was simple and beautiful, and it was totally different from anything any of the other bands had done.

"She's good," Jane whispered to Cooper. "Really good."

When the girl finished there wasn't a sound from the audience. They just stood there, staring at her for a moment as she waited behind the mike. Then they applauded politely, almost nervously, as if they weren't quite sure what they'd just heard. The girl waited, as if she expected the applause to grow louder, and then she turned and walked off-stage. The lights returned to normal and the emcee emerged from the curtains.

"Okay," he said. "That was Voodoo Mama. Could I have all the bands out here please?"

The various bands that had performed during the evening came out from both sides of the stage and met in the middle. Cooper and Jane stood beside T.J. and the rest of Schroedinger's Cat, while another band crowded in behind them. Cooper noticed that the girl from Voodoo Mama was standing across from her. Now that the light was better, Cooper took the opportunity to look at her more closely. She was really pretty. Her mocha-colored skin glowed against the red of her dress, and her long, lean body looked like it had never had an extra ounce of fat on it.

Suddenly, Cooper realized that the girl was looking back at her. She met the girl's gaze and saw that her eyes were an unusual color, a mix of green and brown. She smiled at the girl and received a curt nod in return.

"It's time to choose our winner for tonight," the emcee said. "Who's it going to be, folks?"

People screamed out the names of their favorite bands for a moment, then the emcee held up his hands to quiet them down. "We'll go one at a time," he said. "Your cheers will pick the winner, so when it's your band's turn, make sure you let us hear you."

He pointed to the first band. "Who wants to send Petting Zoo home with the prize?" he asked.

The applause was loud but not overly enthusiastic, even though Petting Zoo's drummer tried to get the crowd pumped up by jumping up and down and waving his arms around.

The emcee moved on to the second band. "How about Stop Motion Photography?" he called out.

This time the applause was much louder and

longer. Stop Motion Photography—SMP for short—was a favorite local band. They played frequently and had a loyal following, and Cooper had noticed a lot of people in the crowd wearing their T-shirts. She also knew that their lead singer, a cocky guy with lots of tattoos, expected to win.

"That's going to be hard to beat," said the emcee as he came to stand in front of T.J. "Can Schroedinger's Cat do even better?"

"Tough break," Cooper whispered to T.J. as the applause came and went without coming close to the enthusiasm the audience had shown for SMP.

Now it was Cooper's and Jane's turn. When the emcee lifted his hand above their heads and said, "Is it time to take your Bitter Pills?" the two of them struck poses, daring the audience to say no to them.

It worked. The crowd went wild. They stomped their feet and clapped, chanting, "Bit-ter Pills, Bit-ter Pills." Cooper looked at Jane and the two of them laughed. This only made the crowd call out their name more loudly. The cheers went on even after the emcee motioned for it to end. When it finally did, Cooper looked over and saw the singer from SMP glaring at her. She winked coolly and blew him a kiss.

"Okay," said the emcee. "Only one more act to go. At the moment, Bitter Pills looks like our winner. Can Voodoo Mama derail their train?"

The girl from Voodoo Mama stood silently, her guitarist standing behind her, looking out at the audience as they applauded her. When it became apparent that she wasn't going to win, she looked at Cooper and the others, seemed to shake her head, and held up her hand, indicating that she didn't care whether they all liked her or not.

What a sore loser, Cooper thought as the emcee walked over to her and Jane and handed them an envelope. "Here's your check for two hundred and fifty dollars," he said. "And when you're ready, there's a main spot on our Saturday night lineup for you."

Everybody walked offstage as the crowd applauded some more. Then the sound system blared to life with music from the club's DJ and everyone began dancing. Backstage, Cooper and her friends congratulated one another on their performances.

"You won this time," said Jed, Schroedinger's Cat's keyboard player and, now that Cooper was gone, new guitarist. "But next time we'll be the ones holding the cash."

"You're on," Cooper said.

"That was quite a song you did," said a voice behind Cooper. She turned around and saw the girl from Voodoo Mama standing there.

"Thanks," Cooper said. "Yours was great, too."

The girl sniffed. "It was too good for this place," she said. "They don't understand jazz."

Well, she's a real charmer, Cooper thought as she stared at the girl. Even her compliments were insults. What was her problem? Was she just mad because she'd lost? Why was she even talking to Cooper if all she wanted to do was be rude?

"Your lyrics were amazing," T.J. said to the girl.

She turned to him and smiled, her mouth slipping from something resembling a frown into a slow, easy grin. "Thank you," she said, looking T.J. up and down. "I think the words are the most important part of a song. I don't like to cover them up with a lot of guitars like some people do." She glanced momentarily at Jane and Cooper as she made her statement, then turned her full attention back to T.J. "I'm Madelaine," she said, holding out her hand.

"T.J.," Cooper's boyfriend said.

When he didn't continue, Cooper elbowed him in the side. "Oh," T.J. said, giving a start. "This is my girlfriend, Cooper, and that's Jane."

"Your girlfriend?" Madelaine repeated, eyeing Cooper. "How interesting."

"Isn't it?" said Cooper, smiling sweetly. If the girl wanted to play games, Cooper was only too happy to give her a run for her money.

Madelaine continued to look at her. "I actually didn't come over here to talk about this silly contest," she said. "I came because I wanted to meet the girl who told the world she was a witch."

Cooper looked at Madelaine, not knowing what to say. She knew that everyone else was waiting for her to speak. Everyone there knew that Cooper was involved in Wicca, but they didn't usually talk about it. Now Madelaine had brought it up as if it were the most ordinary thing in the world.

"Thanks," Cooper said finally. "I think." She wasn't really sure whether Madelaine thought her being into witchcraft was a good thing or a bad thing. Having had run-ins with people who thought it was definitely on the negative end of the scale, she didn't want to have any trouble.

"I read in the paper about what you did," said Madelaine. "You and your friends. I was hoping they might be here as well."

"Good old Amanda Barclay," Cooper remarked caustically. The newspaper reporter had caused her trouble on several occasions. Recently, she'd written a series of articles about Cooper's battle with the school board of Beecher Falls High School after they'd tried to ban her from wearing a pentacle to school. Cooper had successfully stood up to them, and it had made her something of a local celebrity—or a troublemaker, depending on what people thought of her actions.

"My friends couldn't make it tonight," Cooper told Madelaine. "But I'll be sure to tell them we have a fan club."

"I wouldn't call myself a fan," Madelaine continued pointedly. "But I admire your courage."

She never quits, does she? Cooper thought as she nodded at Madelaine. Just when she thought the girl might be trying to make nice, she had to go and say something nasty. There was an awkward silence as no one spoke. Then T.J. said, "I like the name of your band. How did you come up with it?"

Madelaine laughed lightly. "It's what some people call my mother," she said. Then she looked at Cooper again. "You're not the only one who knows something about the spirits."

Before Cooper could reply, Madelaine slipped her arm through T.J.'s. "Now, why don't we go have a soda?" she said, flashing him a smile. "I'm very thirsty."

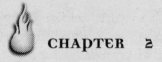 **CHAPTER 2**

"It was the most beautiful thing I've ever seen," Kate told her therapist. "Her parents' ghosts were just holding her. Then they disappeared and Cooper and I hugged her."

She was starting to cry all over again as she remembered the strange events that had occurred on Samhain Eve a few weeks before. She, Cooper, and Annie had performed a ritual in which Annie had called to the spirits of her parents. To Kate's surprise, Mr. and Mrs. Crandall had appeared. It had been an emotional moment, especially for Annie. But it had been very special for Kate, too. Watching Annie finally get to say good-bye to her mother and father, almost ten years after their deaths in a fire, Kate had been reminded of how important her own family was to her. They'd had some rough times over the past few months, and on occasion Kate had wished that she had a different family. But she loved them, even when they were impossible to deal with, and she knew that they loved her. They'd even let her go to the weekly Wicca study class again after meeting some of the instructors. She knew that was a big step for her conservative parents, and she appreciated it.

"Do you really believe that you saw ghosts that night?" Dr. Hagen asked Kate, holding her pencil to her lips as she waited for an answer.

"Sure," Kate said. "We all saw them. We couldn't all have been imagining it."

"Had you and Cooper ever seen photographs of Annie's parents?" asked the doctor.

Kate nodded. "A few," she answered. "Why?"

Dr. Hagen shook her head. "I'm just wondering," she said.

"You don't believe me!" said Kate, surprised. It was the first time she'd ever felt that perhaps the therapist didn't think she was telling the truth. "You think I imagined it all because I wanted it to be true."

"I believe that you had an experience," replied Dr. Hagen carefully. "I'm just not sure I agree completely with your explanation of it."

Kate groaned. "And I thought you were on my side," she said.

Dr. Hagen set her pad and pencil on the little table beside her chair. "I've told you before, I don't take sides," she said. "And I also don't lie. I'm not going to tell you that I think you saw ghosts when I don't."

"Then what *do* you think I saw?" Kate asked her defensively.

"I don't know," admitted the doctor.

"You don't believe in ghosts, though?" Kate prodded.

"I've never seen one," Dr. Hagen told her, not really answering the question.

Kate snorted. "Well, I don't think Annie, Cooper, and I all had the exact same hallucination or something. I *saw* those ghosts. Do you always have to see something before you believe in it?"

"Generally," said the doctor. "Call me old-fashioned."

"I'll see what I can arrange, then," Kate told her.

Dr. Hagen laughed. "Well, before you start sending the Ghost of Christmas Past to wake me up tonight, why don't we talk about how things in the real world are going. How's the situation with your parents?"

"Fine, I guess," Kate said. "We've sort of adopted the don't-ask/don't-tell policy about the whole witchcraft thing. They pretend I'm not really going to Wicca class every Tuesday night and I don't mention anything about it when I get home. It's dysfunctional, but it works for us."

"Hmm," said the doctor vaguely as she picked up the pencil and wrote something on the pad. "And you're okay with that arrangement?"

"As long as I get to go to class," said Kate. She paused. "I guess I would like to be able to tell them *some* stuff," she added. "But it's okay for right now."

"And what about Tyler?" asked Dr. Hagen.

"That's a whole other story." Kate sighed dramatically. "My parents still don't want me to see him. I can't argue with them about it because that would mean talking about the witch stuff some more. But I really want to see him. It's been a long time."

"Do you talk to him?" the doctor queried.

"Sometimes," answered Kate. "He comes to class on Tuesdays when he can, and we talk then. But that's not enough."

"How does he feel about all of this?" the therapist said.

Kate sighed. "I think it bothers him as much as it bothers me," she said. "I try not to talk about it too much because I don't want what little time we *do* have together to be depressing."

"But you don't think he's given up on the relationship?" Dr. Hagen asked. "He's not dating anyone else or anything?"

"No!" Kate said, shocked that the doctor would even suggest something like that. "Tyler? No way. I mean, I know we haven't been the tightest of couples lately, but I know he still loves me. He'll wait until things work out."

"And you love him?" said the therapist.

"Most definitely," Kate replied firmly. "He's everything I could possibly want in a guy."

Dr. Hagen paused as she wrote something down. Kate waited for her to say something, but she seemed engrossed in whatever it was she was scribbling on the paper. Finally, Kate couldn't stand waiting anymore. "So, how do I get them to let me see Tyler again?" she blurted out.

Dr. Hagen stopped writing. "How about asking them?" she suggested.

"They'll just say no," Kate said wearily. "I know they will."

"That's what you thought when I suggested inviting them to a ritual, too," the therapist reminded her. "And you were wrong about that."

"True," Kate admitted. "But I'm not sure they're willing to give in twice in one century. I have to think about it. Thanksgiving is coming up, and my brother will be home from college. That will put them in a good mood. Maybe I'll do it then."

"Holidays aren't always the best occasions for bringing up potentially stressful issues," Dr. Hagen pointed out.

"I know," Kate said. "But I need to tell Kyle about the whole Wicca thing anyway. We haven't talked about it yet, and I feel weird not having him know. I might as well get it all out of the way at once. Besides, once Kyle knows about the class he can help me gang up on Mom and Dad. That's how we've always worked together."

"It would be good to have an ally in the house," agreed the doctor. "Are you fairly certain that Kyle will support you?"

"Oh, yeah," said Kate. "Besides, if he doesn't I'll threaten to tell Mom about the tattoo he got. They don't know about *that* yet."

Dr. Hagen sighed. "Well, I can't officially endorse blackmail as a means to an end, so I'll leave it up to you to work out the ethics of that approach."

"Not that I'm not enjoying talking to you or anything," Kate said, "but how much longer do we have to continue our sessions? My parents brought me here because of the whole Wicca thing. Now that we've gotten that out of the way, is there really any reason to keep spending my Saturday mornings here?"

Dr. Hagen shrugged. "That's up to you, I think," she said. "Do you feel that we've talked about everything you want to talk about?"

Kate was about to say yes, she did think they'd talked about everything. But then she hesitated. While part of her wanted the doctor to tell her parents that everything was fine and that there was no reason for her to keep coming back, another part of her liked talking to Dr. Hagen. She liked being able to say whatever she was thinking, and she liked that the therapist treated her like someone who could make her own decisions. Was she ready to give that up? To her surprise, she found that she wasn't sure she was.

"I'll get back to you on that," she said.

Dr. Hagen looked at her watch. "Perfect timing," she said. "We're done for today."

They stood up, and the doctor walked Kate to the door. "Say hello to your parents for me," she said as Kate left. "I'll see you next week."

Kate left the office and walked to the waiting room, where her mother was thumbing through a magazine and looking bored. "Okay," Kate said. "I know how gripping those articles on bike trips the whole family can enjoy must be, but it's time to get out of here."

Mrs. Morgan put down the magazine and stood up. "For your information, I was reading about the drama on the set of the new Russell Crowe movie," she said as she pulled on her jacket.

"I see," Kate said. "Let me guess—he was moody and didn't like the food?"

"Basically," her mother answered. "But who cares? He's a hottie."

"Mom!" Kate said.

"Please," said Mrs. Morgan as they left the office and walked to the car. "Just because you're married doesn't mean you go blind."

"It's not that," Kate said. "I just thought you'd be more of a Tom Hanks kind of woman."

Her mother laughed. "He's too goofy," she said.

Kate rolled her eyes. She liked joking around with her mother like this. It made her feel more comfortable, the way she had before all of the issues around her involvement in Wicca had put a strain on their relationship. Her mother had always been like a best friend, but that had changed when Mrs. Morgan had found out about her daughter's interest in witchcraft. Since then Kate had missed the way they'd been before.

Now, though, it seemed that maybe things were getting back to normal. Kate attributed this partly to the fact that her aunt Netty, her mother's sister, was doing really well in her battle against cancer, a battle she felt she was winning partly because of the effects of a healing ritual she had done with some of Kate's witch friends. Seeing Netty get better had changed the way Mrs. Morgan looked at witchcraft, and while Kate wished that her aunt never had to fight cancer in the first place, she was happy that some good had come out of it.

Thinking about that reminded Kate that Aunt Netty would be there for Thanksgiving, which was a little more than a week away. Kate hadn't seen her aunt in a while, and she was looking forward to it. She was also looking forward to seeing her older brother, Kyle. It would be great to have the family together for a few days. Now, if she could only find a way to solve her Tyler problem, everything would be perfect.

"What are your plans for tonight?" her mother asked as they drove home.

"Just hanging out with the girls," Kate replied evasively. She knew her mother was still a little unsure of her friendship with Annie and Cooper, so she tried to bring them up as little as possible. If she didn't say *which* girls she was hanging out with, her mother could assume whatever she wanted to. Not that there were a lot of other options when it came to who she might be spending time with. These days, Cooper and Annie were pretty much it for Kate as far as really close friends went.

Mrs. Morgan nodded but didn't say anything. Kate quickly started talking about something else, and for the rest of the ride home they stuck with subjects that didn't have the potential for turning into arguments. Kate had gained some ground over the past few weeks, and she didn't want to lose it by pushing too hard.

Later that evening Kate walked over to Annie's house and knocked on the door. It was opened by Annie's little sister, Meg. When she saw Kate she frowned. "You're late," she said seriously. "Everyone else is already here."

"I'm sorry," said Kate, trying not to laugh as she looked at the younger girl's solemn expression. Although Meg was only ten, she sometimes acted like someone ten times her age.

"It's okay," Meg said as Kate came inside. "We haven't started yet."

Kate walked into the kitchen, where she found Annie, Cooper, and Sasha seated around the table drinking hot chocolate and eating cookies.

"*There* you are," Annie said. "We thought you weren't going to make it."

"Now I see where you get it from," Kate said to Meg, who had followed her into the kitchen and was helping herself to a cookie. "I'm only ten minutes late," she added to the others.

"Well, now that you're here we can start

cooking," Annie said, standing up. "Who wants to do what? We need someone to cook the pasta, someone to chop stuff for the sauce, someone to make a salad, and someone to make the cheesecake."

"I'll do pasta," Cooper said instantly. "I can't possibly get that wrong."

"I'll chop," said Sasha.

"I'll take salad duty," Annie said. "That leaves Kate and Meg on the cheesecake. Can you guys handle that?"

Kate looked at Meg. "What do you think?" she asked. "I've never made one."

"No problem," replied Meg. "Just follow me."

Kate laughed as everyone got busy. She watched as Meg got out a mixing bowl and started assembling ingredients from the refrigerator.

"Wow," Kate said as she watched Meg at work. "You really do know what you're doing."

"Annie and I make cheesecake all the time," said Meg. "Just get me the sugar. It's in that cupboard up there and I can't reach it."

"So, what has everyone been up to?" Sasha asked as she diced some chili peppers. "Any news about your parents, Coop?"

"No," Cooper answered. "They're still separated and no one is really saying anything. But we all went out for dinner the other night and there was no fighting, so I think that's a good sign. And last night Jane and I won that battle of the bands thing we entered."

"Congrats," Kate said. "I'm sorry I couldn't go."

"Me, too," chimed in Annie. "I had to stay home with you-know-who."

"Hey!" Meg protested. "I'm right *here*."

"Is your aunt having a good time in San Francisco?" Kate asked Annie.

"I haven't heard anything yet," answered Annie. "But my guess is that she's having a *great* time. She and Grayson have been talking up a storm. She tried to convince me she was only going down there for business, but I know better. I think she's really falling for him."

Grayson Dunning was a writer Annie and her aunt had met while they were in San Francisco the month before. He and his daughter, Becka, lived in the house where Annie, Meg, and her parents had lived before her parents' deaths. He and Aunt Sarah had clicked—really clicked—and the two of them had been talking a lot since then.

"You should hear her on the phone with him," said Meg, sounding as if the thought of it revolted her. "She sounds like Annie did when that *boy* used to call her."

Nobody said anything for a moment. The boy Meg was referring to was Brian, whom Annie had dated over the summer and into the beginning of the school year. He'd been her first real boyfriend, and she'd really liked him. But he'd dumped her after she wrote an editorial for the school paper about being involved in Wicca. Her friends knew it was still a sore subject with her, and usually they didn't bring it up.

"Speaking of boys," Cooper said, quickly changing the subject. "Someone tried to steal mine from me last night."

"T.J.?" Sasha said. "Who put her hands on your man?"

"Just this girl at the club," Cooper replied. "She was one of the singers. Afterward she was all over T.J. I think she was just mad that we beat her."

"What was she like?" Annie inquired.

Cooper shrugged. "I don't know," she said. "Pretty. Great voice."

"Sounds like you'd better be careful," commented Sasha.

Cooper laughed. "Can you imagine T.J. cheating on me?" she said. "That would be like Tyler cheating. Neither of them would do that. They just don't have it in them."

"Ow!" said Annie.

The others turned to look at her. She was at the sink, holding her finger under the running water.

"What happened?" Kate asked her.

"Oh, I just cut myself a little," Annie said. "I was slicing tomatoes and the knife slipped."

Kate wondered what had distracted Annie, ordinarily so adept in the kitchen. What had they been talking about? T.J. and Tyler. *She must have been thinking about Brian*, Kate told herself. She looked at Annie, who was drying her hand and looking at the cut.

Kate felt sorry for her. *She'd make such a great girlfriend*, she thought. Brian had really lost out. It was too bad he had freaked out over the witch issue. But there was someone out there for Annie. Kate was sure of that. After all, Kate had found Tyler, and she'd never thought she could find a guy who was almost perfect.

She smiled happily to herself as she helped Meg pour the cheesecake batter into a pan. *That's what Annie needs*, she thought. *She needs someone like Tyler.*

CHAPTER 3

"Well, what's the news?" Annie asked Becka excitedly.

It was Sunday morning. The phone had just rung, and Annie had picked it up thinking that it was her aunt calling. But it had been Becka. Annie was actually happier to hear Becka's voice on the other end of the line. That meant she could find out what her aunt was *really* up to.

"They've spent the whole weekend together," Becka said breathlessly. "They went to the symphony on Friday, a play last night, and they just went to brunch before Dad drives her to the airport. I'm telling you, this is serious. I've *never* seen him act like this with anyone. Oh, and she invited us there for Thanksgiving."

"She did?" Annie said, surprised. Thanksgiving was the most important family holiday they celebrated. Christmas, with its memories of the deaths of Annie's parents, had always been something of a sad time of year. But Thanksgiving was another story. Annie, Meg, and Aunt Sarah always made a big deal out of it, spending all day in the kitchen together cooking and watching the Macy's parade on TV. Occasionally, they invited people to join them for dinner, but only really special people. If her aunt had invited Becka and her father, that meant she really was serious about him.

"It will be great to see you," Annie told Becka. "You can meet Cooper and Kate and the rest of my friends. I think you'll really like them."

"I'm looking forward to it," Becka said. "It's so weird how all of this happened, isn't it?"

"It sure is," agreed Annie. "It's almost like my parents' ghosts were trying to bring us all together or something."

She paused for a moment, then asked Becka, "You haven't had anything happen in the house, have you?"

"Not since the ritual we did," Becka replied. "In fact, Dad's having a hard time writing the new book in the series, and he says it's because the ghosts are gone."

Annie laughed. Grayson Dunning wrote a series called *The Changeling*, about a girl who was descended from faeries. It was one of Annie's favorite series, and she still couldn't believe that the author was dating her aunt. Mr. Dunning had been attracted to Annie's former home because of the stories about it being haunted, and he said having ghosts there inspired him to write.

"We'll have to find him some new ghosts," quipped Annie. "You should have Dixie come over and see what he can do." Dixie was a witch, an outrageous figure who liked to dress up like Glinda the Good Witch from *The Wizard of Oz*. He had helped Annie perform a ritual in the Dunning house to help her parents cross over to the other side. It hadn't worked—at least not completely—but Dixie had been very helpful, and Annie was happy to have made another Wiccan friend.

Annie glanced at the clock. "I have to go," she said. "I'm meeting a friend of mine. Meg is over at a friend's birthday party, so I actually have the day to myself."

"Is it a date?" Becka asked curiously. "You sound excited about it."

"Oh, no," Annie said. "It's not a date. Not really. No."

"Okay," Becka said, sounding suspicious. "Well, have fun. And call me when your aunt gets home. I want to hear what she tells you."

"Will do," Annie said. "Bye."

She hung up and ran upstairs to get dressed. She only had half an hour, so there wasn't much time. What should she wear? She opened her closet and looked at the things hanging up. None of them seemed quite right. She gave up and went to her dresser, pulling open the drawers and pawing through piles of shirts. Finally, unable to come up with anything fabulous, she slipped into a pair of jeans and a black turtleneck. Then she looked at herself in the mirror.

"Well, it's not going to get you on the cover of *Vogue*," she said. "But it will have to do."

She ran downstairs, grabbed her jacket, and left the house. With a little bit of luck, she would get the bus and be downtown just in time. As she walked briskly toward the corner and the bus stop, she tried not to think about what she was doing. If she did, it just made her even more nervous.

She was relieved to see that the bus was pulling in as she reached the stop. She got on and took a seat. As she rode through town, the thoughts in her head went one way and then another. First she wondered where things between her aunt and Mr. Dunning were going to go. Then she thought about what Cooper had said the night before about T.J. and the girl who had shown an interest in him. She wondered how Cooper had really felt about knowing that the other girl was attracted to her boyfriend. Cooper had seemed okay about it, but Annie wondered if she really was worried that T.J. might leave her for someone else. How could Cooper be so sure that T.J. would never cheat on her?

She looked down and realized that she was rubbing the spot where she'd cut herself the night before. She'd put a bandage on it, and now she was running her finger across the thin plastic strip that circled her left index finger. Beneath it she could feel the sore spot where the skin was knitting back together. *Yes*, she thought. *I wonder how Cooper would feel?*

The bus came to her stop and she got off. The November afternoon was sunny but cool, and she put her hands in her pockets to keep them warm as she walked the two blocks from the bus stop to the coffee shop that was her final destination. She paused outside the door, taking a deep breath, and then went inside. She scanned the room until she found who she was looking for, then walked over and sat down.

"Hi," she said.

"Hi," Tyler replied. "I just got here, so your timing is perfect."

Annie smiled. She looked at Tyler. He was also wearing jeans and a black turtleneck. "We match," she said.

Tyler looked down, then looked at her. "So we do," he said.

Annie looked around the coffee shop. It had just opened a few weeks ago, and she had never been there. Instead of the usual boring tables and booths, it was filled with sofas, big armchairs, and lots of small tables. It was more like sitting in a living room than in a restaurant. There was even a big fireplace with a crackling fire in it. If she hadn't been so nervous, she would have felt like curling up in the big couch she was sitting on and reading a favorite book.

A waitress walked over and handed each of

them a small menu. Annie looked it over and said, "I'll just have the hot cider."

"I'll have the chai with cinnamon," Tyler told the woman.

She left to get their drinks. Neither Annie nor Tyler said anything for a minute. Then Annie cleared her throat and said, "Thanks for coming."

Tyler nodded but didn't say anything.

"I know it's a little weird," continued Annie. "I haven't really known what to say to you about—well—you know. About what happened."

"You don't have to say anything," Tyler said.

"Yeah, I do," Annie told him. "I shouldn't have kissed you like that."

"Really, it's okay," said Tyler again. He sounded nervous, and Annie wondered if the situation was as difficult for him as it was for her. She didn't know how it could be. After all, she had been the one who had kissed him. He hadn't done anything at all.

"It was just that we'd been spending so much time together," Annie explained. "I was having a great time."

"So was I," Tyler told her, smiling so that his chin dimpled.

Annie tried not to think about the way Tyler's black hair curled over his forehead, or about how beautiful his golden eyes were. She looked down at the bandage on her finger as she spoke.

"I don't know," she said. "Maybe it was because of what happened with Brian. Maybe it's just that you're the only really great guy left on Earth."

Tyler laughed. "That's certainly not true," he said.

"Of course it is," Annie contradicted him. "You're really great."

"I didn't mean that part," said Tyler, grinning at her. "I meant about me being the *only* great guy. I'm sure there are at least two of us."

Annie smiled. She knew that Tyler was trying to make her feel better about the stupid thing she'd done. She appreciated that. Of course, it only reminded her of how nice he really was, and that made her feel depressed all over again. She sighed.

"I feel so dumb," she said.

Tyler reached across and took her hands in his. Annie found herself wanting to pull away from him, but she didn't. She felt his fingers rubbing against hers, and all she could think about was how nice it felt. Even the cut on her finger stopped hurting as he stroked her skin.

"You're not dumb," Tyler said gently. "You're a wonderful person."

"How wonderful is it to kiss your best friend's boyfriend?" Annie asked him.

Tyler gave her a look. "Stop beating yourself up," he told her. "Like you said, we'd been spending a lot of time together. And it's not as if Kate and I have been doing that lately."

"That's still no excuse," Annie replied. "Let me let you in on girl rule number one—you don't kiss someone else's guy. Not unless you're trying to cause trouble or have a starring role as the girl everyone loves to hate on a weekly drama."

Tyler laughed. "I don't think anyone could ever hate you," he said.

There he goes again, Annie thought. Once again she thought about the conversation she and Tyler had once had about how people were surprised that he and Kate were an item. Tyler had remarked that Annie was more like the kind of girl he'd always pictured himself being with. As much as she wanted to forget that he'd ever said that, she couldn't. More than anything, she wished that Tyler had never said it. As weird as it was to admit it, things would be a lot easier if she knew that Tyler would never think about being with someone like her. But she knew that he *would*, and that thought haunted her like the voices of her parents once had.

Tyler let go of her hands as the waitress came and set their drinks down. Annie quickly picked up her mug of cider, just in case Tyler had been thinking about taking her hands again. She couldn't bear to have him do that, not when she knew that he could never be hers.

"Let's make a deal," Tyler said, sipping his chai. "You stop beating yourself up over this and I'll try to stop being so darn appealing."

Annie rolled her eyes. "That comment just knocked you down a notch already," she said. "Keep it up and I won't even want to *talk* to you."

"Good," Tyler said. "Now that that's out of the way, let's move on to a new topic. What's going on with the crew?"

Annie brought him up to speed on the latest news. "And that's about it," she said when she was done.

"You're like a walking CNN news brief," Tyler remarked. "I can tune in once a week and find out everything I need to know." He paused. "I feel sorry for Cooper," he said. "I know what it's like having your parents separate."

"She seems to think they'll work it out," Annie said.

"I hope so," replied Tyler. "And it sounds as if your aunt and this new guy might turn into something interesting."

"I don't know," Annie said, drinking the last of her cider. "But speaking of her, I should get going. Meg's party will be over soon, and I want to clean the house up a little before Aunt Sarah comes home."

"I'll walk you to the bus," Tyler said.

Annie started to put some money on the table but Tyler held up his hand. "I'll get it," he said. "You can buy the popcorn the next time we go to a movie."

They put their coats on and left. Walking to the bus stop didn't take very long, and soon they were standing on the corner. Annie turned to Tyler. "You should probably go," she said. "This is how I got in trouble the last time, remember?"

"Good point," Tyler said. "So we're cool, right?"

"Right," Annie said.

"Good," said Tyler. "Then, is it safe for me to hug you good-bye?"

"I think I can handle that," Annie told him.

He reached out and pulled her to him, hugging her tightly for a moment and then letting go. "I'll talk to you later," he said, and walked away.

Annie watched him go. As she looked at his retreating back she thought, *I am so* not *handling that*. She'd lied to Tyler. Having him hug her like that had brought all of the feelings she had for him rushing to the surface. She sighed. What was she going to do? She didn't know. But whatever she did, she couldn't let Tyler know that she still had it bad for him. He thought she was over it, and that's what counted. She was just going to have to suffer in silence.

The bus came and she got on. All the way home she replayed over and over again in her mind the way Tyler had held her hands. She closed her eyes and pictured his face. She knew it was exactly the wrong thing to do, but she couldn't help it. She leaned against the window and tried to will the image of his face out of her mind, but it wouldn't go away. *I am the worst person in the entire known universe*, she thought miserably.

CHAPTER 4

"We've just passed the seven-month point of our journey," Sophia said as she stood in front of the weekly Tuesday night Wicca study group. "Five more to go."

"And a day," Cooper reminded her.

"And a day," repeated Sophia, nodding her head and laughing. "We can't forget that. Now I think you'll all agree that this time has gone by pretty quickly."

Cooper thought about that. True, it did seem like the dedication ceremony they'd done had been only a few weeks ago. But actually it had taken place back in April. Now, it was almost winter. During that time a lot had happened, both to her personally and to the group as a whole. They'd all matured in their knowledge of magic and of witchcraft. Strong friendships had been formed. Cooper thought of Sophia, Archer, and the other teachers as her extended family. And Kate and Annie had become like sisters to her, largely because of what they'd gone through together. Most important, she'd learned a lot about herself and her abilities.

"As you know," Sophia continued, "at the end of the year and a day many of you will be asked if you want to be initiated into Wicca as full-fledged witches."

Cooper felt a thrill of excitement go through her when she heard Sophia's words. A full-fledged witch. It sounded to Cooper like some kind of baby bird that had finally gotten its wings and could fly on its own. But she knew that undergoing formal initiation was a very serious step. It was a big commitment. It meant dedicating herself to Wicca for probably the rest of her life. Deciding whether or not she was ready for that was something she was going to have to do pretty soon. But did she know enough to make that decision?

"As you all know by now, the form of witchcraft you've been learning here in class is only one of the ways the Craft is practiced," Sophia told them. "There are many other ways. Some of them are similar to ours with only a few differences. Others are very different. And witchcraft itself is part of the larger world of pagan religions, some of which are a lot like Wicca and a lot of which are completely unique. The members of my coven and of our sister coven, the Coven of the Green Wood, believe that it's important for people to experience and understand as many different paths as possible before deciding on one. So, for the next month we're going to ask each of you to spend time in another tradition."

Cooper looked at Annie and Kate. What was Sophia talking about?

Sophia held up a black velvet bag. "In this bag are slips of paper, each one with the name of a different kind of faith written on it. Each of you will select a slip. You will spend the next month learning about the path you choose. We want you to find out as much as you can in that time. In particular, we would like you to see how the path you choose is similar to and different from the one you're on now."

"What happens if we find out we like the new path better?" asked a man sitting beside Cooper.

Sophia smiled slyly. "We've had that happen in the past," she said. "And that's perfectly all right. The point of this exercise is to expand your knowledge of the different paths. You all came to this class because you were interested in finding out what Wicca is all about. You found something you liked and you decided to study it some more. It's entirely possible that the same thing will happen to you again. Don't be afraid of that. As we've discussed many, many times before in this group, there are many ways of exploring the world. This is just one of them."

"I'm not sure I like this idea," Kate whispered to Cooper and Annie. "I'm happy with what we're doing."

"I don't know," Annie said. "It might be fun."

"Who wants to choose first?" Sophia asked.

"I will," Cooper said, standing up.

She walked up to Sophia, who opened the bag. Cooper reached inside and picked a slip of paper. Unfolding it, she read, "Celtic shamanism."

She immediately felt afraid. Her mind raced back to Midsummer Eve, when she had entered a cave with the group of kids who had ended up chasing her through the woods. They'd told her that the cave had been used by shamans who wanted to have visions. Their leader, Spider, had pretended to put her through some kind of vision-inducing ceremony. Only it had all been an elaborate trick to make her look foolish. Looking at the slip in her hand, she was reminded of the horror of that night all over again.

"I don't know if I can do this," Cooper told Sophia. "Can I pick another one?"

"If you really feel you can't do it, you can pick another one," Sophia answered. But as Cooper began to put the slip back into the bag, Sophia added, "But remember that sometimes challenges come our way for a reason."

Cooper paused and looked at her. "That was low," she said. Sophia knew very well that Cooper could seldom resist a challenge. Now she was making Cooper feel that if she returned the slip to the bag she would be admitting defeat. She withdrew her hand. "I'll keep this one," she said.

Sophia's eyes twinkled. "Don't worry," she said.

"We have some great books that will help you out."

Cooper returned to her seat as Annie stood up and walked forward. When she removed her slip and read it a curious look came over her face. "As-a . . . . As-a," she said. "Ah-sa-true?"

"It's pronounced ow-sah-tru," Sophia told her.

"What is it?" Annie asked, perplexed.

"It's the Norse religion," Sophia told her.

"Norse," Annie said. "As in Freya and the gang?"

"That's right," Sophia confirmed.

"Great," Annie said, sounding as if her choice was anything but.

Cooper knew that her friend was thinking about her recent experience with aspecting the Norse goddess Freya. Freya's personality had mixed with Annie's with some disturbing results. When Annie returned to where the girls were sitting, Cooper said, "It looks like we're both having reunions with the ones that gave us the most trouble."

"I wonder where that leaves me?" Kate said. "I suppose I should find out."

She stood up and went to Sophia. As she reached into the velvet bag she felt a sense of apprehension. What was she going to pick? Unlike Cooper and Annie, Kate hadn't had any negative experiences with any particular magical traditions, so she wasn't afraid of choosing any specific path. But she was also very aware that the exercise was meant to challenge them, and her experience with magical challenges was that they were sometimes very difficult.

Her fingers touched the slips of paper. She stirred them around, waiting to see if any of them called to her. Finally she just grabbed one and took it out. She unfolded it and looked at what was written there. "Santeria," she said.

"A very interesting one," remarked Sophia.

"I've never heard of it," Kate said.

"Don't worry," Sophia reassured her. "We'll point you in the right direction."

Kate went back to her friends. As the rest of the class went up and selected their slips, they talked about their choices.

"This sounded fun at first," Cooper said. "Now I'm not so sure."

"I certainly didn't think I'd be seeing Freya again this soon," remarked Annie.

"I don't even know what mine is," Kate said. "At least you guys have a clue."

"I guess we'll all find out soon enough what's in store for us," Cooper told her friends. "Whatever it is, it's sure to be interesting."

"Famous last words," Kate said.

For the rest of the class they talked a little bit about the different traditions they had chosen. Sophia gave all the students books to get them started and let them spend some time reading. Kate, Cooper, and Annie sat together looking over the materials they'd been given and discussing what they found.

Sophia walked around the room, talking to each of the class members. When she reached the three girls she sat on the couch they were gathered around. "How's it going?" she asked.

"This Asatru stuff is pretty grim," Annie said, shutting the book she was holding in her lap. "It's all about honor and duty and being loyal to the clan."

"It can be a little warriorlike," Sophia agreed. "But try to see past that to what the people who practice Asatru find appealing about it. That's really what this exercise is all about."

"I think I might just like this shamanism stuff," Cooper told Sophia. She'd been reading a book about the various shamanistic practices.

"There's a really good exercise for doing a vision quest in that book," Sophia told her. "Check that out. Kate, how are you doing?"

"I'm still confused," Kate admitted. "There's a lot of information here."

"Let me see if I can help you out a little," said Sophia. "What is it you're confused about?"

"I can't even really tell what Santeria is," said Kate unhappily.

"That can be difficult to determine," Sophia told her. "Basically, Santeria is a variation on the traditional African religion of Yoruba. The two share many similarities. But Santeria has been heavily influenced by Cuban culture and the practices of other Latin peoples."

"Okay," Kate said. "But what's all this about saints and spirits?"

"The Yoruba religion is based on the worship of

certain spirits, called orishas," Sophia explained. "Santeria also focuses on these spirits."

"But these pictures show Catholic saints," Kate said, showing Sophia a photograph of a Santeria shrine in the book. "I recognize a lot of these from church."

Sophia nodded. "That's right," she said. "You see, the Yoruban religion first made its way to America when African people were brought here as slaves. Their new masters didn't want them practicing their religions because they thought it gave them too much power. So the slaves masked their rituals and practices by assigning the different orishas to corresponding saints."

"So the slave owners thought they had given up their religion?" Cooper said.

"Right," said Sophia. She took the book from Kate and turned to a photo of a statue decorated with flowers and beads. "For example, this is a statue of Saint Barbara. Only it's not Saint Barbara who's being worshiped here. It's the Yoruban orisha Chango, the god of war and thunder."

"This is all really confusing," Kate said. "I don't know how I'm going to figure it all out."

"You're in luck," Sophia told her. "There's a woman in town who is a Santera, a priestess of Santeria. She also happens to be a friend of mine. She runs a botanica."

"A what?" asked Annie.

"A botanica," Sophia explained. "It's a shop where they sell items used in the practices of

Santeria and Yoruba. They tend to be the focal points of the communities who practice these religions."

"And this woman will talk to me?" Kate asked.

Sophia nodded. She took a piece of paper and wrote on it. "Here's the address. You can stop in to her shop when you get a chance."

Sophia moved on to the next group of students, leaving the girls alone. Kate looked at the paper Sophia had given her. Then she looked at Cooper and Annie. "I'm not sure I can go to this place," she said. "It sounds a little weird."

"What's so weird about it?" asked Annie.

Kate shrugged. "I don't know," Kate said. "All this stuff about the saints and these spirits, I guess."

"It's no weirder than what we do here, probably," Cooper told her.

"I know," admitted Kate. "But I'm used to this."

Cooper took the paper from Kate and looked at it. "Botanica Yemaya," she read. "I know where this is. It's over by one of the used CD places T.J. and I go to a lot. Tell you what. We'll go with you." She looked at Annie. "Okay?"

"Sure," Annie said. "It will be like a field trip. Besides, I think it sounds really cool. I'd love to see this botanica."

"And this woman," Cooper added. "Listen to her name—Evelyn LeJardin. I wonder what she's like."

"All right," Kate said. "We'll all go. When?"

"How about tomorrow after school?" Cooper suggested.

"That's fine with me," said Annie.

"Kate?" Cooper asked.

"Yeah," replied Kate. "That works for me."

"I wish there was some kind of Asatru store or something I could go to," said Annie. "It doesn't look like there's a lot of information about it."

"Why not just call up your good friend Freya?" suggested Cooper, grinning.

"Very funny," Annie said. "Keep that up and I'll aspect Thor and see what happens."

"Hey there," someone said.

The girls looked up and saw Tyler standing next to them.

"I thought I'd stop by and say hello," he said.

Kate jumped up and gave her boyfriend a hug. "Hi," she said. "I feel like I haven't seen you in forever."

"Not quite forever," said Tyler. "But almost. Hi, Cooper. Hi, Annie."

"Hey," said Cooper.

Annie just waved. Cooper looked at her friend. Annie had turned a funny shade of pink. "Are you okay?" Cooper asked her. "You look flushed."

"It's just really hot in here," Annie said. "I think I'll walk around a little."

She stood up and walked quickly toward the front of the store. Cooper got up. "I think I'll get some air too," she said. "You two try to behave yourselves."

She left Kate and Tyler to catch up and went

after Annie. She found her looking at a display of crystals.

"What's up?" Cooper asked.

"Nothing," Annie said.

Cooper folded her arms across her chest. "Come on," she said. "Something is going on. What is it?"

"What makes you think something is going on?" asked Annie defensively.

"Oh, I don't know," replied Cooper. "Maybe because when you saw Tyler you turned the color of cotton candy."

"I was just hot," insisted Annie.

"Liar," said Cooper teasingly. "Now, spill it. You know something, don't you?"

"Know something?" Annie repeated, sounding genuinely surprised. "Know something about what?"

"Tyler," said Cooper. "What is it? Is he going to break up with Kate? Is that it?"

"What?" said Annie. "Why would you think something like that?"

"You've been spending a lot of time with Tyler," Cooper explained. "I just thought he might have said something to you. I mean, don't you think it's odd that he happened to show up here tonight?"

"He probably just wanted to see Kate," Annie answered.

"Maybe," Cooper said. "But I still think you know something."

"I don't," Annie said, shaking her head. "I don't know anything."

Cooper looked at her for a minute. "If I didn't know you better I'd swear you and Tyler were having an affair," she said.

"Right," Annie said. "That's *exactly* what we're doing. Tyler's come to tell Kate that it's over and that he's running off with me. I didn't want to be there when it all went down, so I came out here to hide."

"Look at you being all sarcastic," said Cooper. "Fine. If you don't want to tell me, that's okay. I'll find out eventually. I have my ways."

"There's nothing to find out," Annie said. "Really."

Annie picked up a crystal and examined it intently. Cooper wanted to interrogate her some more, but she resisted the urge. She was sure that Annie knew something about Tyler and Kate. But whatever it was, Annie wasn't ready to talk about it. That was okay, though. Cooper could wait. And eventually she *would* find out.

CHAPTER 5

"There it is," Annie said, pointing across the street to a store that had BOTANICA YEMAYA painted in blue letters across the big glass window.

It was raining, a cold heavy rain that had begun falling in the early afternoon and hadn't let up. The streets ran with rivers of water that carried leaves and garbage to the storm drains, and there were puddles everywhere water could collect. Cooper, Kate, and Annie waited for the light to change, their hands in their pockets and their jackets pulled tightly around them.

The light switched from green to yellow to red, and the three girls crossed the street quickly, anxious to get out of the weather. Cooper pushed open the door of the botanica and they stepped inside. The interior was warm and dark and smelled like incense. A glass counter stretched across the back of the shop, and behind it were shelves filled with jars of herbs and powders. A case to the right held tall candles in many different colors. And everywhere else they looked there were statues. Some of them were statues of saints. Others were unfamiliar to the three of them.

The store was lit by soft lights and by many candles which flickered along the top of the glass counter. They lent an air of cheerfulness to the store, especially in contrast to the storm outside, but they also made it seem mysterious. The flames cast shadows on the faces of the statues, which stared out at the girls as they stood in the store looking around at everything.

On a small table near the entrance to the store there sat what looked like a small head made out of concrete. It was about the size of an orange, and it had eyes, a nose, and a smiling mouth made out of cowrie shells. Scattered on the table in front of the head were several wrapped candies in shiny cellophane wrappers, as well as an unlit cigar and a small glass filled with dark brown liquid. Kate walked over to the head and reached out to touch it.

"Papa Elegba does not like to be picked up," said a voice from the back of the store.

Kate withdrew her hand quickly and turned around. Coming out from a doorway behind the glass counter was a woman. She was a little taller than Kate was. Her long black hair was braided and tied with blue and white ribbons, and she wore a loose blue dress that flowed around her. Around her neck hung several necklaces made of multi-colored beads, and on her wrists were heavy copper bracelets. As she stepped forward, Kate saw that she was barefoot.

"I'm sorry," Kate said. "I didn't mean to touch it—I mean him," she added, remembering that the woman had called the head by a name.

The woman nodded. "No harm has been done," she said, smiling slightly. "Can I help you?" Her voice had an unusual accent to it, a soft lilt that suggested strength as well as kindness.

"We're looking for Evelyn LeJardin," Kate told her. "We're taking a class at Crones' Circle, and our teacher sent us here. Well, she sent me. My friends came with me."

"I am Evelyn LeJardin," the woman answered. She walked to where the girls were and held out her hand. Kate took it. The woman closed her fingers around Kate's in a firm grip. "Welcome."

"I'm Kate," Kate told her. "This is Cooper, and this is Annie."

Annie and Cooper each shook Evelyn LeJardin's hand. She nodded to each of them in turn, then looked back to Kate. "Sophia tells me that you wish to learn something about Santeria," she said.

Kate nodded. "Yes," she said. "We're in the Wicca study group, and we've each been assigned a different path to learn about. I chose Santeria."

"I see," said Evelyn. "Although perhaps it is more accurate to say that Santeria chose you, no?"

Kate wasn't sure how to respond. "Maybe," she said, feeling stupid.

Evelyn laughed. "Come," she said, waving at the three of them. "We will talk back there."

She turned and padded to the rear of the store. Kate followed, with Cooper and Annie behind her. Evelyn stepped behind the counter and the three girls stood in front of it. "Now, what would you like to know?" she asked Kate.

"I don't know, really," Kate answered. "I've done a little reading on Santeria, so I know something about it. I guess what I'm really curious about is how you got into it."

Evelyn turned and pointed to a picture that sat on a shelf behind her. Colored beads hung around it and a small white candle burned in front of it. Scattered on the shelf was an assortment of objects, including a bottle of perfume, a deck of playing cards, a china kitten, and some flowers.

"That is my mother," Evelyn said, indicating the woman in the photograph. "She was a priestess of Santeria. As was her mother before her and her mother before her. We lived in New Orleans, but originally my family came from the West Indies. It was there that they learned the religion."

"So you were raised in it, then?" Kate said.

Evelyn nodded. "Yes," she replied. "Myself and my sisters. My mother was quite famous in New Orleans, and many people came to her."

"What did she do for them?" Kate asked.

"Many things," answered Evelyn. "Healed their children. Divined the future. Helped them find husbands and wives."

"Do you do those things, too?" Cooper asked her.

Evelyn raised an eyebrow. "Why?" she asked. "Are you looking for a husband?"

Cooper laughed. "No," she said.

"Well, when you are you come to me," Evelyn said authoritatively. Then she looked at Kate again. "Yes, we do all of those things," she said. "But that is not what the religion is really about. It is about serving the orishas, the spirits who make things possible."

"And what does that mean, exactly?" Kate queried. "From what I've read, it seems like a lot of time is spent making the orishas happy."

"It is," Evelyn said, nodding vigorously. "They can be very demanding, the orishas. But very generous, too, to those who serve them well."

"Who are the orishas?" Annie asked. "I haven't read as much as Kate has," she added hastily.

"The central figure in the religion is called Oloddumare," Eveleyn explained. "He is what others might call God, Allah, or Yahweh. The orishas serve Oloddumare, and they are many things," Evelyn explained. "Some believe they were created by Oloddumare to serve him. Some believe that they were once humans who became gods. Others see them as the spirits of nature. Each one plays a different role in life."

"Sort of like the Greeks had gods and goddesses?" asked Annie.

"Yes," said Evelyn. "Something like that. For example, the orisha Chango is the god of thunder and lightning. The orisha Oshun is the goddess of rivers and of beauty. But they are more than just these things. They each represent a powerful human emotion. Chango represents the driving force within us. Oshun is the personification of the force of love. My own orisha, Yemaya, represents divine motherhood, as well as oceans."

"What do you mean when you say that Yemaya is *your* orisha?" Kate asked Evelyn.

"Practitioners of the religion believe that we are each assigned a specific path in life," Evelyn answered. "At birth each of us is chosen by an orisha who helps us along that path. During our lifetimes we may work with all the orishas, but there will always be one who guides us and protects us above all others. We are considered the 'children' of that orisha."

"How do you know who your orisha is?" Cooper asked her.

"There is a special ceremony that is done to determine that," Evelyn told her.

"So, Yemaya is your orisha?" said Kate.

"Yes," Evelyn confirmed. "I am a child of Yemaya. I am also a priestess of Yemaya, as I have been initiated into her mysteries."

The front door of the shop opened and a young woman came in, interrupting the conversation. She walked up to the counter and spoke to Evelyn in

Spanish. They conversed for a few minutes and then Evelyn nodded and turned to the shelves behind her. As the girls watched, she pulled down several different jars and poured some of the contents into plastic bags. She then fetched a yellow candle and added it to the pile on the counter, along with a small bottle of a pinkish liquid. Evelyn put everything into a bag and handed it to the woman, who slid some money across the counter to her. Then she nodded at Evelyn and the girls and left the shop.

"Can I ask what that was all about?" Kate asked Evelyn tentatively.

"She has a problem that requires fixing," Evelyn responded. "I told her to perform certain rituals, and I gave her the tools she needs to do them."

"Like working a spell?" Annie suggested.

"Something like that," Evelyn answered. "Followers of the religion do not usually think of it as magic. They ask the orishas to help them, and in return they provide the orishas with things they desire. The ritual that woman will do is meant to please the orisha Oshun. She hopes that if Oshun is pleased with her then she will offer her help in the matter at hand."

"Do you consider yourself a witch?" Kate asked.

Evelyn shook her head. "No," she said. "I know that there are similarities between what witches do and what we do, but I do not consider myself a witch. I do not think that what I do is magic, although some do call it that. Santeria means 'the worship of the saints,' and that is what we do. We worship the orishas and, through them, Oloddumare. Perhaps we sometimes ask them to do certain favors for us, but I do not think of that as magic."

"But in what I read about Santeria it says that people who follow it can make things happen by doing what seem like spells," Kate said. "One of the things I remember is a ritual for getting an enemy to stop talking about you. It involved sewing up a beef tongue or something like that."

"That is correct," Evelyn said. "There are rituals such as that one. Again, though, the person performing such a rite would ask one of the orishas for her or his help in the matter."

"This is really interesting," Kate said. "It sounds like Santeria has a lot in common with Wicca, but it also sounds really different in a lot of ways. I wish I could see an actual ritual so I could understand it better."

"Perhaps you can," Evelyn told her. "This Saturday I am hosting a celebration gathering. If you would like to come I would welcome you."

Kate looked at Cooper and Annie, both of whom nodded eagerly.

"We'd love to," Kate told Evelyn.

"It is done then," she replied.

"Is there anything special we need to do?" Kate asked.

"Just come with open hearts and open minds," Evelyn said. "We will do the rest. The ritual will take place here, in the back of the store. Be here at eight o'clock."

"We will," Kate told her. "And thank you again for talking to me. I really appreciate it."

"Not at all," said Evelyn. "And let me give you some things to read so that you will understand more what is going on." She reached beneath the counter and took out several small books, which she slipped into a paper bag and handed to Kate. "On the house," she said, waving away Kate's hand as Kate fished in her pocket for some money. "I have a daughter your age, and I like to see young people interested in such things."

"Will your daughter be at the ritual on Saturday?" Kate asked. "I'd like to talk to a young person who is involved in Santeria."

"She will be there," Evelyn said. "And I'm sure she will enjoy speaking with you."

The door to the store opened again. Evelyn looked up and smiled. "Ah, Maddy," she said. "We were just speaking about you."

Kate turned around and saw a girl about her age walking in. Like her mother, she wore her hair in numerous braids, but the ribbons that tied them were maroon and white rather than blue and white. The girl came up to them and stopped.

"This is my daughter, Madelaine," Evelyn said. "This is Kate, Annie, and Cooper."

"Well, hello again," Madelaine said, looking at Cooper coolly.

"Hello," Cooper replied curtly.

"You two know each other?" Kate asked, surprised.

"We have done battle," replied Madelaine.

When Kate looked confused, Cooper said, "Madelaine was one of the singers in the battle of the bands."

Suddenly, Kate understood Cooper's response. *That must be the girl who was flirting with T.J.*, she thought.

"Kate and her friends are coming to the party on Saturday," Madelaine's mother explained.

"Are they?" Madelaine said, sounding amused.

"I was hoping I could talk to you about your experiences in Santeria," Kate told the girl.

"I would be happy to talk to you," Madelaine replied.

"Your mother has told us a lot already," said Kate. "Are you also a child of Yemaya?"

Madelaine laughed. "No," she said. "I am an Oya." She indicated the ribbons in her hair. When Kate seemed confused she said, "Yemaya's colors are blue and white, which is why my mother wears them. Oya's colors are maroon and white."

Kate nodded. "And what is Oya the orisha of?"

"Death," Madelaine said.

Evelyn sighed. "My daughter has always been slightly dramatic," she said. "Orisha Oya is indeed the goddess of death. But more than that, she is the goddess of change. She is fierce and wild, and when she dances her skirts kick up the winds of change that cleanse our lives of dust and debris and sweep them clean again so that we can move forward."

"That, too," Madelaine said.

"Well, I look forward to seeing you on Saturday," said Kate. "Thanks again for everything."

The girls said their good-byes and left the store. It was still raining, so they walked briskly to the bus stop. As soon as they were away from Botanica Yemaya, Cooper said, "I can't believe it's that girl."

"She seemed okay," Kate commented.

Cooper snorted. "Only because her mother was right there," she said. "You should have seen her at the club."

"Did T.J. show any interest in her?" Annie asked.

"Of course not!" Cooper said. "I mean, he *talked* to her, but that was it."

"Then why are you so mad about it?" continued Annie.

"Because she's just—just—just," Cooper said, as if she was searching for the right word.

"Kind of like you?" suggested Annie.

"Oh, right," said Cooper.

"Well, she is," Annie insisted. "She's pretty. She's confident. You said she sings really well."

"Yeah, but—" said Cooper.

"But nothing," said Annie. "She reminds you of you, and you're jealous of her because she likes your boyfriend."

Cooper didn't say anything.

"I'm right," Annie said smugly to Kate. "You can always tell because she runs out of things to say."

"Fine," Cooper said. "So she's pretty and confident and sings well. I think those are enough reasons to hate her."

Annie and Kate laughed.

"Well, how would you like it if someone was after *your* boyfriend?" Cooper demanded.

"I don't have a boyfriend anymore," Annie reminded her.

"And I would never worry about Tyler," said Kate. "So it's not a problem."

"Goddess, the two of you pretend to be so well adjusted," said Cooper, pretending to be annoyed. "It makes me sick."

"Speaking of getting sick, we're all going to catch our deaths of pneumonia if we keep walking in this rain," Kate said.

"There's the bus," Annie replied, nodding toward the corner, where a bus was pulling up like some big lumbering beast moving slowly through the downpour.

The three of them made a mad dash for it and got there before the bus pulled away. It was the rush hour commute, and the bus was more crowded than usual. They got on and headed for the back, stepping over the umbrellas and shoes of the dripping wet people who were crammed on. There were no free seats, so the three girls stood holding on to the overhead rail as the bus pulled back out into traffic.

"Even if you don't like Madelaine, I think Saturday night will be interesting," Kate said to Cooper. "I, for one, am looking forward to it."

"I hope so," Cooper replied. "Hey, by the way, what did Tyler have to say last night? You never told us." Cooper looked at Annie pointedly, but Annie pretended to be looking at something outside the window.

"He just wanted to stop by and say he misses me," Kate said. She sighed. "He's such a great boyfriend. I don't know what I would do without him."

"It's a full moon tonight," Annie said suddenly, as if she'd just remembered that.

Kate and Cooper looked at her oddly.

"I just thought you should know," she said. "In case you want to do any rituals or anything."

"Okay, then," Cooper said. "Thanks for the heads-up."

"Are you okay?" Kate asked Annie. "You're kind of red."

"Great," said Annie. "I mean, I *feel* great."

The bus reached their stop and they got off. They walked as quickly as they could through the rain, and when they got to the corner where they went their separate ways they parted, waving good-bye to one another and then each hurrying home in a different direction.

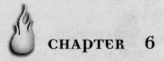

CHAPTER 6

Tyler grabbed Annie and pulled her to him. She could feel his heart beating against hers. She could smell the clean scent of his skin. She could sense his breath against her cheek as he held her tightly. She'd waited for a long time to have him hold her that way, and she didn't want him to ever let go.

"I know I shouldn't be doing this," he whispered in her ear. "But I can't pretend anymore. I love you, Annie."

"What about Kate?" Annie asked, afraid of what the answer might be.

"What I feel for you is different," Tyler said. "I can't really explain it. It's almost as if we were a couple before. Maybe in another lifetime. I think you're the person I was destined to be with."

Annie opened her eyes and sighed. "You can't even have a fantasy without making it sound like a soap opera," she told herself.

She was in her bedroom, curled up in bed. She was wearing her favorite flannel pajamas and she was rereading the first book in Grayson Dunning's Changeling series. She'd read it three times before, but she never tired of it. Plus, now that she knew him personally, it was even more fun to imagine him writing the books.

It was still pouring outside. The moon was hidden behind the storm clouds, so her full-moon ritual had been something of a bust. In the end she had done a simple meditation and then gotten into bed. The rain pattered on the roof steadily, and the sound had lulled her into sleepiness. Before she'd known it, she was thinking about Tyler again.

"You have *got* to stop doing that," she admonished herself sternly. "Tyler is Kate's boyfriend. There will be another guy for you."

Still, it *had* been kind of nice thinking about him. She couldn't deny that. She just wished she could stop feeling guilty. After all, she hadn't really done anything to be ashamed of. Yet whenever anyone mentioned Tyler around her she got all weird, like they'd be able to see that she had a thing for him just by looking at her face.

She picked up the book that she'd put down earlier. She began reading, trying to get back into the story. But she couldn't. She'd get through half a page and then she'd start thinking about Tyler again. By the time she turned the page, she'd have forgotten everything that had happened and have to start all over. Finally she put the book down and got out of bed.

Walking to her desk, she picked up the book that Sophia had given her about Asatru. She went back to bed, slipped between the sheets, and pulled the comforter up. She opened the book and began reading.

She was finding her introduction to the Norse religion very interesting. She'd read stories about the goddesses and gods before, but she hadn't known anything about the actual religion that was built around them. It was fascinating to learn how the celebration of the religion was so closely tied to the day-to-day lives of the people. It wasn't just something they did one day a week, or on special days. It was what they did every day. In that respect, it reminded her a lot of Wicca.

But she was also a little bit troubled by what she was reading, particularly the reference to loyalty to one's friends. What would the ancient Norse people have thought about a girl who fantasized about making out with her best friend's boyfriend? That certainly didn't show a lot of loyalty on her part to Kate. So why couldn't she stop thinking about Tyler? It wasn't as if he was encouraging her or anything. It was all her own doing.

She put down the book, turned off the light, and snuggled down into the warm sheets. The rain danced over her head as she yawned and drifted into sleep. But just as her thoughts were fading into dreams the phone beside her bed rang, startling her awake. Instinctively, she picked it up and answered it with a sleepy, "Hello?"

"Hi, Annie," said a guy's voice. "It's me. Tyler."

Suddenly she was wide awake. She sat up in bed. "What's wrong?" she said.

"Why does something have to be wrong?" Tyler said.

"I'm sorry," Annie said. "It's just that when the phone rings this late at night I'm always convinced that it's bad news."

"Is it too late?" asked Tyler, sounding embarrassed. "I can call you tomorrow."

"No!" Annie said. "It's okay. What's up?"

"I just wanted to see if you could meet me tomorrow," Tyler said. "There's something I want to talk to you about."

"Um, sure, I guess," said Annie. "What time?"

"How about four-thirty?" replied Tyler. "At the wharf?"

"Okay," Annie told him. "I'll be there."

"Thanks," Tyler said, sounding happy. "I'll see you then."

He hung up, leaving Annie listening to a buzzing dial tone. As she set the receiver down she realized that she'd forgotten to ask Tyler *why* he wanted to see her. He'd said that he wanted to talk to her about something. But what? She almost picked up the phone and called him back to find out, but she stopped herself. That would just look weird, and she wanted him to think that she was totally over her momentary indiscretion. Calling him—even for what she thought was a good rea-son—might make her look all clutchy.

That didn't stop her from *thinking* about what he might have to say to her, however. A million differ-ent things ran through her mind, all of them ending with Tyler grabbing her and kissing her. She was hopeless, and she knew it. *Probably, he just wants to ask your advice on what to get Kate for Yule*, she told herself. After all, it *was* only a little more than a month away. She herself had already been thinking about what to get her friends for the holiday. It would make sense that Tyler, who unlike other boys actually *thought* about what he should get his girlfriend, would be thinking along the same lines.

With a sigh Annie got back into bed and closed her eyes again. The call from Tyler had woken her up, but the rain pattering on the roof above her coaxed her back asleep with its steady song.

After school the next afternoon, Annie took the bus downtown to the wharf. She hadn't men-tioned to either Kate or Cooper that she was going. But it wasn't like Kate didn't know that Annie and Tyler hung out together. She did, and she was okay with it. That didn't make Annie feel better though, so she just kept quiet about the whole thing.

When the bus reached the downtown area she got off and walked to the wharf. The rain had stopped and it was sunny, although the fall after-noon was coming to a close and the shadows had started to lengthen. She loved this time of the year, when the seasons changed and the world felt as if it was slowly falling asleep for its long winter rest. Even the ocean looked like it was growing quieter, the waves rolling in slowly and sliding onto the beach as if they had all the time in the world.

Tyler was standing on the end of the wharf, leaning over the railing and looking down at the water. The afternoon sun glinted off his hair, and as Annie walked toward him she wished she could have a picture of him just standing there, staring out over the ocean.

"Hey," she said when she reached him.

Tyler turned around and smiled at her. "Hey."

Annie leaned against the railing beside Tyler, purposefully not letting her arm touch his. The two of them stood there silently, looking at the water for what seemed to Annie like the longest minute in the world.

"Sorry again about waking you up last night," Tyler said.

"Really, it was okay," Annie said. "I wasn't really sleeping. I was just listening to the rain."

"I love hearing the rain on the roof," Tyler said. "Especially at night. And it's even better in a tent. A couple of summers ago we went to this big pagan gathering where we stayed in tents. It rained a lot, and it was great hearing it outside while we were inside, dry. Do you like camping?"

"Um, I've never really been," Annie answered.

Why was Tyler going on about camping? she wondered. Not that she minded hearing him talk or anything, but he seemed to be rambling. It wasn't like him at all.

"The ocean is really beautiful right now," Tyler said.

Annie nodded but didn't say anything. Had Tyler asked her to meet him just to talk about rain and the ocean? He didn't seem to be in any hurry to tell her why he *had* called her. Did he just want to hang out? That was okay, but he'd said that he had something he wanted to talk to her about.

"What are your Thanksgiving plans?" Tyler asked her.

"Mr. Dunning and Becka are coming," she told him. But she was sure that she'd already told Tyler that. Had he forgotten?

He nodded. "We're doing the usual coven get-together," he said. "It should be fun."

Okay, Annie thought. *This is weird. Is he ever going to tell me what's up?* Then a horrible thought occurred to her. What if Tyler had brought her there to tell her that he didn't think they should hang out so much? What if he'd decided that her obvious crush on him was too much? Maybe that's why he was acting all strange around her. Her heart sank. That was it. He was going to tell her to back off. Well, she would save him the trouble.

"I've been thinking . . ." she began, but at the same time Tyler turned to her and said exactly the same thing. They looked at one another for a moment and then laughed.

They both paused, looking at each other. "What have you been thinking?" Annie asked, unable to stand him staring at her that way.

"I've been thinking," Tyler began again. But again he stopped.

Here it comes, Annie told herself, preparing to hear Tyler tell her that their hanging out together was a bad idea. But still he didn't say anything. He just stood there, looking at her. She tried to look away from his golden eyes, but she found herself looking right into them, wondering what Tyler was thinking about.

He opened his mouth to say something and then stopped. Finally he said, "I've been thinking that sometimes I think too much."

Then he leaned forward and kissed her. Annie didn't have time to think about it. One moment she was staring into Tyler's eyes and the next his mouth was on hers. Before she could register any of it he had pulled away and was standing there looking at her, his hands gripping her arms.

Was she dreaming again, or had Tyler just kissed her? It had all happened so quickly that she wasn't even positive that she hadn't imagined it all. All she could do was stand there feeling slightly dizzy as Tyler's beautiful golden eyes searched her face.

"I'm sorry," he said, dropping his hands and stepping back. "That was way out of line."

Annie shook her head, still unable to speak. She wanted to tell him that it wasn't out of line, that she had wanted him to do it. But her thoughts were all jumbled together. This was Tyler. It wasn't just some guy. It was her best friend's boyfriend. He wasn't supposed to be kissing her. He was supposed to be telling her that he didn't want to see so much of her.

"I'm just going to go now," Tyler said. "We'll just pretend that I didn't do that, okay?"

He was backing away, a hurt and confused look on his face. Annie, stunned, could only watch him and shake her head. She wanted to speak, but her voice was locked inside of her.

"No," she whispered hoarsely as Tyler continued to go. "No."

Tyler was moving away from her now. He turned around and started to walk more quickly. He was leaving. She couldn't let that happen.

"No!" she called out, forcing the sound from her throat.

She ran after Tyler. Hearing her call out, he turned around. Annie ran to him and stopped just in front of him. She was afraid to touch him, in case he pulled away, so she just looked into his eyes.

"Annie, I'm sorry," he said. "I didn't mean to—"

"Then why did you?" she asked.

Tyler looked away for a moment, then looked back. "I think about you all the time," he said. "I try not to, but I do."

Annie felt her lip beginning to tremble. She bit

it so that she wouldn't do something dumb, like cry.

"I know I'm not supposed to think about you like this," Tyler continued. "And to tell the truth, I'm not exactly sure why I *do*. Ever since you kissed me that night at the bus stop. Or maybe even before that."

He stopped and took a deep breath. "Wow," he said. "This is really hard."

He reached out and took Annie's hands in his, holding them tightly. They were standing very close together. Annie hoped he would hug her again, but she was terrified that if she stepped into his arms he would pull away from her. She wouldn't be able to bear that. She just knew it.

"I don't know what to do about this, Annie," Tyler said gently. "I really don't."

"What do you *want* to do about it?" she asked him.

Tyler shook his head. "I don't think I can answer that," he told her. "Not right now. I'm really confused."

Annie nodded. "I know how that feels," she said.

"All I know right now is that I really like spending time with you," said Tyler. "You make me feel comfortable, and your friendship means more to me than I can tell you. You're smart and you're funny and—" His eyes shone in the sun as he looked at her and smiled. "And I think you're really beautiful," he added.

Annie's heart was beating wildly as she listened to Tyler talk. It was just like her fantasy, only better.

She couldn't believe it. Was he really saying all of those wonderful things to her? Was he really holding her hands and looking at her with those gorgeous eyes of his?

Then a thought passed through her mind, eclipsing her joy like a cloud passing over the sun.

"But what about—" she started to say.

"Don't," Tyler interrupted. "Not now."

Annie looked down. How could she not think about Kate? How could *Tyler* not think about Kate? It wasn't possible. But she wished she *could* forget that she was standing there listening to her best friend's boyfriend tell her that he— She couldn't finish the thought. What *was* Tyler telling her anyway?

"What happens now?" she asked him.

He shook his head. "I don't know, Annie," he said. "I'm not exactly thinking clearly, you know?"

Annie sighed. "Oh, I know," she agreed.

Tyler pulled her closer. His face was only inches away from hers. "I don't know what comes next," he said. "But I know that right now I can't let you go before I do this again."

His mouth closed over hers. This time she let herself feel the kiss. She'd imagined it so many times that it almost felt as if she were dreaming it again. But this time when she reached up to feel Tyler's face in her hands she touched real skin, not empty air. Her fingers touched the smoothness of his cheek, the roughness where the short hairs of his unshaven beard tickled her. And she felt his tongue, warm against her lips. These things were real. And she knew that when he finally stopped kissing her and pulled away she would be looking once more into those magical amber eyes.

She didn't know what was going to happen when the kiss was over. She knew that there were questions to be answered, and she knew that she might be making the biggest mistake of her life. But as Tyler's hand caressed her back, those fears slipped away and all she knew was that she'd never wanted to be with someone so much in her life.

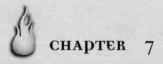

CHAPTER 7

"Are you going to be like this all night?" Kate asked Cooper.

"Like what?" snapped Cooper. "I'm fine."

Kate nodded. "Right," she said. "You always sit hunched in your seat with your arms across your chest. You'd look less defensive if you were wearing a full suit of armor."

Cooper sat up in the bus seat and put her hands in her lap. "Happy?" she asked sarcastically.

"You didn't have to come if you didn't want to," said Kate.

"I want to," Cooper said. "I just wish *she* wasn't going to be there."

"She kind of has to be," remarked Annie. "It's her mother who's holding the gathering."

"Besides," added Kate, "it's not like there's any chance whatsoever of her getting T.J., is there?"

"No," Cooper said after a minute of edgy silence. "I guess there isn't."

"Then, try to have a good time," said Kate. "I

think it's going to be really interesting, don't you, Annie?"

"Sure," Annie said brightly.

Kate looked at her two friends. They were both acting a little strangely. Cooper was being all weird and jealous about Madelaine, and Annie seemed to be in perky overdrive. Kate didn't know what was up with the two of them, but she wasn't going to spend a lot of time worrying about it. She had other things or. her mind, like Tyler. She really missed him lately. Their brief meetings at Crones' Circle just weren't enough. She was going to have to find a way to see more of him. Her parents had been in good moods recently, and she knew that once Kyle arrived on Tuesday for the Thanksgiving break they would be even happier. If she was going to ask them for permission to see her boyfriend, that was the time to do it. She'd have to think that through later, though. Right now the bus was stopping.

"Come on," she said, standing up and waving Annie and Cooper ahead of her.

The three of them got off and walked to Botanica Yemaya. The store was closed for the night, but Evelyn had told them to ring the bell. Kate pressed it and waited. A minute later the door opened and Madelaine's face peered out. She smiled when she saw Kate, Cooper, and Annie standing there.

"Ah," she said. "You came. Come in."

The three girls walked into the store, and Madelaine shut the door behind them. Kate saw that she was wearing a white dress with a full skirt. Her feet were bare, and she had a ring of small bells tied around one ankle.

"Come with me," said Madelaine, leading them through the door at the back.

They passed through and found themselves in a large room. One end of it was apparently used as a stockroom. Boxes and shelves lined the wall, and there were bags of herbs and cartons of candles and other items piled around. But the main area was clear. The wood floor had been swept clean, and there were lit candles on tables arranged along the sides of the room. The tables were also piled high with food. Bowls and platters seemed to be everywhere, and the air was rich with the scent of roasted meats, sweet baked things, and spices that Kate couldn't identify. Just smelling them made her mouth water, and she found herself hoping she would get to sample the food before too long.

Against one wall was what looked like an altar. It was a large table covered in white and yellow silk. On top of it was a statue of a woman, and around her feet were piled pumpkins, bottles of wine, and plates of little cakes. Yellow and white flowers were heaped around the table as well, and there were candles of the same colors burning on either side of her.

"Who is that?" Annie whispered to Kate.

"I don't know," she answered. "I guess we'll find out."

Kate looked around. There were a number of

other people already gathered in the room. Like Madelaine, most of the women were wearing white dresses, while the men had on white pants and shirts. But other people were dressed in regular clothes, so Kate didn't feel like she and her friends were completely out of place.

To one side of the room, several men were playing hand drums. They knelt on the floor with the drums between their knees, and their hands tapped out rhythms on the tops. They seemed to be practicing, as they would play for a minute and then stop, laughing and talking.

"Hello there."

Kate looked up and saw Evelyn walking toward them.

"Hi," Kate said, smiling at her. "This looks like a big party."

Evelyn laughed. "It is," she said. "This is a celebration marking an important day for one of my godchildren."

"What do we do?" Annie asked.

"Just watch," Evelyn told her. "I will be busy, so Madelaine will explain things to you as they happen. If you have any questions you may ask her."

Evelyn walked away, leaving Kate and the others with Madelaine. She turned to them and said, "You are very lucky. We do not usually let people of the eleventh rank attend our ceremonies."

"Eleventh rank?" Cooper said guardedly. "What's that?"

Madelaine looked smug, as if she enjoyed the fact that they didn't know what she was talking about. "In Santeria there are twelve ranks of people," she said. "The first are the *omokolobas*. They are very powerful priests who have received initiation into the highest mysteries. The twelfth and lowest rank are those who do not believe in the orishas or in Santeria. In between are those who have attained various levels of initiation and understanding."

"And why are we in the eleventh rank?" Kate asked with interest.

"I give you the benefit of the doubt when I say that," Madelaine replied. "Those of the eleventh rank believe in Santeria and the orishas but have not received any of the initiations. You *do* believe in the orishas, do you not?"

Kate was taken aback. "I suppose I do," she said. "I've never really had any experience with them."

Madelaine laughed. "Perhaps that will change tonight," she said.

"What level are you?" asked Cooper, clearly annoyed at the girl's haughtiness.

"That is considered a rude question to ask," Madelaine told her. "However, since you are not of the religion, I will not be offended."

"Gee, thanks," Cooper remarked.

Madelaine ignored her and continued. "I am of the seventh rank," she said. "I am called an *aleyo*, which means that I have received certain of the initiations and mysteries. When I receive the *asiento*, then I will be a santera."

"The *asiento*?" said Annie. "What is that, some kind of tool or something?"

"No," Madelaine said. "It is a ceremony—the most important ceremony most people will undergo in the religion. It means 'making the saint,' and it is when you are initiated into the mysteries of your guardian orisha."

"When will you do that?" Kate asked her.

"When my *madrina* believes I am ready," she said.

"You mean your mother?" said Annie.

"A *madrina* is the person who performs the first initiations on a person," Madelaine answered. "In this case, yes, it was my mother. But she is even more important as my *madrina* than as my mother. She is my spiritual godmother."

"Your mother said that tonight was a celebration for one of her godchildren," Kate said. "Is that what she meant?"

"Yes," Madelaine confirmed. "My *madrina* has many godchildren. Tonight we are celebrating the anniversary of the *asiento* of one of them. His name is James. Two years ago he was initiated into the mysteries of Oshun."

"Isn't Oshun a woman?" Cooper asked.

"It does not matter," Madelaine said. "The orishas don't care what sex you are. James is an omo-Oshun, meaning a child of Oshun. Tonight we will celebrate her."

"I take it that's Oshun," Kate said, nodding toward the statue on the altar.

"That's right," said Madelaine. "She is the orisha of love and beauty. Her colors are yellow and white."

All of a sudden the drummers began to play in earnest. Madelaine motioned for Kate, Cooper, and Annie to follow her. "We are beginning," she said.

They walked with her over to the side of the room, where the other people gathered for the celebration were all standing. There was an air of anticipation in the room, and Kate found herself feeling both nervous and excited as she waited to see what would happen next.

The drummers continued to play, the steady rhythms filling the air with sensuous sound. The people standing began to sway to the music. Some stamped their feet, while others clapped. Kate wondered if the songs meant anything in particular or if the drummers were just making them up.

As the drummers played, Evelyn entered the room. She moved slowly and gracefully, passing by the people and scattering something on the floor from a bowl she carried in her hand.

"What is that?" Kate asked Madelaine.

"Ground corn," she was told. "It is to cleanse the room."

Evelyn made a circle around the room, scattering the corn and saying something that Kate couldn't hear. Although the ritual was different from any she had attended, she couldn't help but think that what Evelyn was doing was similar to casting a circle. Something about her actions felt familiar, and as she finished making her circle Kate felt as if they were now all standing in sacred space.

"Welcome to my home," Evelyn said to the assembled guests as the drummers stopped playing. "Tonight we are here to pay tribute to Oshun, who has blessed my *ahijado* James. Please join me in welcoming the orishas who will visit us tonight."

The drumming began again as Evelyn began dancing. The people around Kate also began dancing, slowly moving their feet and sometimes clapping their hands. Kate found herself moving to the music as well, although not as vigorously as some of the others. She still felt a little awkward. She glanced at Cooper and Annie and noticed that they, too, were holding back.

Then a woman broke away from the group and walked to the center of the room. She stood there, her hands on her hips, staring at the others in what seemed almost a hostile way. A moment later she began dancing, stepping confidently and throwing her head back.

"It is Oya!" Madelaine said excitedly. "Oya has arrived."

"What do you mean?" Kate asked her, confused.

"The drums call to the orishas," said Madelaine. "When they come they inhabit the body of one of their children so that they can join the party. That is

Lucy, an omo-Oya like me. Oya has chosen her to ride tonight."

"Ride?" repeated Annie, who was listening to the conversation.

"Like a horse," explained Madelaine. "The orishas ride their children. Lucy is not Lucy right now. She is Oya. Watch."

Kate looked on while Lucy continued to dance. Her movements were sure and almost fierce, and the expression on her face was one of pride and determination. She really did look like some kind of goddess, and Kate wondered if it was true that the orisha was really controlling the woman. Was that possible? She thought about Annie, and how she had once taken on the characteristics of the goddess Freya after invoking her in a ceremony. Was this the same thing?

As Lucy moved around the floor she was joined by a man who walked quietly away from the group and stood, facing them, with his head lowered. He moved slowly and gracefully, swaying to the drums as his hands clapped gently. Then he raised his hands above his head and looked up. There was a serene expression on his face.

"Papa Obatala!" cried several people.

The man held out his hands and beckoned to those who had called him. They rushed forward, touching him.

"What are they doing?" Cooper asked Madelaine as they all looked on.

"That is Obatala," Madelaine explained. "He is one of the most beloved orishas. They go to him for blessings."

"So they really believe that man is Obatala?" Cooper said.

"He *is* Obatala," Madelaine insisted. "I would recognize him anywhere."

Kate looked at Madelaine. Something about her face had changed. She no longer seemed so stuck up. She was smiling at the man she called Obatala, and she looked happy. *She really does believe it's him*, Kate thought. *But how can she be so sure?*

Her thoughts were interrupted by a deep laugh. Looking around, Kate saw a short, heavyset woman break away from the group around Obatala and begin doing a funny dance where she set first one foot and then the other on the ground, stamping like a big, heavy bear. The expression on her face was comical, as if she were trying to appear scary. She laughed again.

"What have you for Oggun?" she cried out in a low voice.

"The orisha of iron and weapons," Madelaine said to Kate and the others. "He's one to watch."

Someone walked up to the woman and offered her a lit cigar, which she took and immediately began puffing on, blowing big clouds of smoke around. The dancers fanned the smoke around their heads.

"Oggun loves cigars and rum," explained

Madelaine. "It is considered lucky to have his smoke touch you."

As if hearing her, the woman turned her attention to the four girls standing at the side of the room. Walking as if she were much larger and heavier than she really was, the woman strode over to them and stopped. She looked at each one in turn, puffing on her cigar and eyeing them critically. When she looked at Kate she took the cigar out of her mouth.

"My child," she said. "Why have you not come to embrace me?"

Kate looked at Madelaine. "Me?" she said, surprised.

The woman nodded. "I recognize you as an omo-Oggun. Come to me, child."

The woman held out her hands, the cigar still hanging from her mouth. Kate didn't know what to do, but Madelaine urged her forward. "Go," she whispered. "He will not hurt you."

Kate stepped forward. The woman wrapped her arms around Kate and suddenly she found herself lifted high in the air. Kate was shocked at how strong the woman was, and couldn't believe that she had the strength to lift her so high. Yet the woman's grip was sure, and Kate felt no danger as the woman hoisted her up and down three times before setting her back on her feet. Then the woman took the cigar from her mouth and blew a large cloud of smoke into Kate's face. Kate breathed it in, surprised to find that it didn't choke her.

"Do not forget me the next time we meet, child," the woman said in her strange, rough voice. "Oggun has blessed you."

"Thank y-you," Kate stammered, not knowing what else to say.

The woman nodded and walked away, stopping to greet some other people who had come to ask for Oggun's blessing.

Kate looked at Madelaine and saw the girl looking at her with a strange expression. "What?" Kate asked.

"That was most unusual," Madelaine told her. "The orisha marked you as one of his children."

"What does that mean?" Annie asked her.

"You should speak to my mother when the ritual is over," Madelaine said. "She will tell you more."

Kate looked at her friends. The encounter with Oggun had left her feeling both excited and frightened. What did it mean? Why had Oggun called her one of his children? She wasn't a follower of Santeria. Before that week she had never even heard of it. How could she possibly have any connection with one of its gods?

It was probably just a mistake, she told herself. Clearly the woman was having some kind of spiritual experience, but why had she singled out Kate to talk to? It was all too weird. She was sure that Evelyn would tell her to just forget about it.

For the next hour the dancing continued. Several

other orishas arrived and took over the bodies of the dancers, but none of them approached Kate or spoke to her. Finally, at the end, Oshun came. As Madelaine explained it to them, she was the guest of honor and therefore was the last one to arrive and dance. When she came she appeared in the body of a beautiful woman dressed in yellow. She went immediately to James and embraced him. He offered her several gifts, which she admired and placed on the table near her statue. Then she took some of the food that had been laid out for her and offered it to the people around her, who took it eagerly.

"That food is considered blessed by the orisha," Madelaine told Kate and the others. "It is very lucky to eat it."

The ritual continued for a while longer with dancing and drumming. Then, one by one, the orishas departed. The people they had been "riding" collapsed on the floor, and were helped up by those around them. Once back on their feet, they looked around as if they had been asleep and just woken up. Then they smiled and laughed as their friends told them how they had behaved. Kate thought that they all looked incredibly happy. She saw the woman who had picked her up, and part of her wanted to ask her if she remembered doing it. But she thought that would be rude, so she didn't.

"Well, what did you think?" Evelyn asked as she came over to where Kate and the others were standing.

"I'm not sure I understood it all," said Kate.

"Papa Oggun recognized her as one of his," Madelaine told her mother.

Evelyn raised an eyebrow. "Is that so?" she asked.

"That woman picked me up," Kate told her. "Then she blew smoke in my face."

"Not she," Evelyn corrected her. "He. Oggun. It was not Esperanza who picked you up. It was Oggun." She smiled broadly.

"What does it mean?" asked Kate. "She—I mean he—said I was his child. But this is not my religion."

Evelyn nodded. "Even so, the orishas may be with you," she said. "And Oggun . . . that is very interesting. We will talk some more about this, I think. But for now I must go attend to my guests. You will come and see me?"

"Sure," Kate said.

Evelyn embraced her, then gave hugs to Annie and Cooper. "Good night," she said.

Madelaine showed them out, saying good night at the entrance to the store. As they walked back to their bus stop Kate thought about what had happened.

"Do you guys think that was for real?" she asked Annie and Cooper.

"Did it *feel* real?" Annie replied.

Kate thought for a minute. She had definitely been lifted into the air by someone who shouldn't have been strong enough to do it. *That* had felt real. But she knew that wasn't what Annie meant. Then she thought about the way the woman had looked at her. Even though the features had been those of a middle-aged woman, the eyes had belonged to someone else. They had looked at Kate with recognition, and with a sense of love. But had they been Oggun's eyes? Had she really come face-to-face with one of the orishas of Santeria?

"Yes," she said after a moment. "It felt real."

CHAPTER 8

"It was weird," Cooper told Jane the next day as they sat in Jane's bedroom playing around on their guitars. "Incredibly weird."

"What was so weird about it?" Jane asked, knitting her brow as she tried to play a difficult chord progression she'd been working on all afternoon.

"I don't know," Cooper responded. "I guess the way everyone just seemed to accept that the orishas were really inside those people. They didn't even question it."

"But you do?" asked Jane.

"It just seems too easy to fake," said Cooper. "Not fake, really, but too easy to convince yourself that it's real. How do they know those people aren't just really into it and think the orishas are riding them?"

Jane shrugged. "Does it make a difference?" she said.

"Of course it does," Cooper said defensively. "What good is it if they're all just pretending?"

Jane stopped playing. "Some of the stuff you've told me that *you* do would sound pretty weird to people who didn't understand it," she remarked.

"I know," Cooper said. "But I've experienced it, and I know it's real."

"Do you?" said Jane. "How do you know *you* aren't just convincing yourself it's real?"

Cooper thought about the question. "It's something you feel here," she said, touching her stomach. "You just know the energy is really flowing."

"Maybe that's how those people feel about it, too," suggested Jane. "What do you think they would think if you told them that you talked to a ghost?"

"Point taken," Cooper replied. "I guess I would really like to believe that we were talking to actual orishas, but I have this mental block about it."

Jane nodded. "I heard this rabbi once who said that people like what they believe to be hard to prove. That way no one can convince them that it's not real."

"Makes sense," said Cooper. "Maybe that was what made me skeptical—it seemed weird that these gods and goddesses would just show up at a party and act like real people."

"But isn't that how you're supposed to think of them?" asked Jane. "When you do a ritual and you invite some deity into the circle, don't you feel like she or he is really there?"

"Sometimes I do," Cooper answered. "But I don't think I'm as good at it as a lot of people are."

"You probably just need practice," said Jane.

"Speaking of which, I haven't even tried any of the exercises in that book Sophia gave me to read," said Cooper. "We're supposed to talk about what we've learned so far at class this week."

"Why don't we do one of the exercises now?" asked Jane. "I can help you with it."

Cooper looked at her doubtfully. They were supposed to be practicing their new songs.

"Come on," Jane pleaded. "I've never had a friend I could do magical stuff with. This will be fun."

"Okay," Cooper said, putting down her guitar. She opened her backpack and took out the book she'd been reading, *The Shaman's Journey*. Opening the book, she turned to one of the exercises she'd been looking at but hadn't yet tried.

"This one is all about discovering what your totem animal is," she told Jane. "Shamanism has a lot to do with entering the different spirit worlds. The shamans believe that when they enter a world sometimes they'll be met by a totem animal that will guide them. The animals represent different things and have different abilities. The exercise helps you meet your particular animal."

"Sounds cool," said Jane. "What do you do?"

"It's a guided meditation," Cooper told her. "You read it and I do what you tell me."

"I like *that*," Jane joked.

"Do you mind if I stretch out on your bed?" Cooper asked. "You're supposed to be lying down."

"Be my guest," Jane told her.

Cooper lay down on the bed, putting her hands at her sides. Jane sat in a chair opposite her.

"Just read the meditation," Cooper said.

Jane studied the page for a moment while Cooper relaxed by closing her eyes and breathing deeply. Cooper had never done any kind of ritual work with Jane, although Jane had been studying Wicca a little bit on her own for a while. She didn't know how the two of them would work together. But this was a good way to find out. A meditation was a relatively easy thing to do. Plus, she trusted Jane and felt comfortable with her, and for Cooper that was always half the battle. She worked well with Annie and Kate because she knew she could trust them.

"Are you ready?" Jane asked.

"Whenever you are," Cooper said.

"You're standing at the beginning of a path," Jane read in a clear, calm voice. "It's twilight. The sky above you is fading into night, and all around you the shadows are growing. The path runs toward a hill, but you can't see exactly where it goes. You set foot on the path and begin walking."

Cooper pictured the scene as Jane described it. She saw herself in a meadow, following a path that had been mown through the tall grass. As she walked the wind rippled the grass on either side of her, and she could feel it tickling her hands as she passed through it.

"Follow the path as it winds around the hill," Jane instructed her. "It winds around and around it in a spiral. As you walk you are climbing the hill, going to the top."

In her mind, Cooper climbed the hill. Jane's voice led her, calling her forward. She felt her mind slipping into a tranquil state, and she knew the meditation was beginning.

"When you reach the top of the hill it is night," Jane told her. "The sky is clear, and there are thousands of stars above you. In front of you is a tree. Half of the tree is on fire. Its leaves burn brightly, but it is not consumed. The other half of the tree is in full leaf, green and alive. Birds nest in its branches, singing."

Cooper could see the tree just as Jane described it. It looked like a massive oak tree, towering over her with its strong branches reaching out. It seemed impossibly huge—the biggest tree in the world. On the right side it was covered in a coat of flame, the red and yellow tongues flickering in the night. The other side was untouched, and from its many rustling leaves came a song that was sweet and filled with happiness.

"Go to the tree," Jane read, and Cooper pictured herself stepping forward. "Here you will see three doors in its trunk. These are the doors to the three realms. Choose one of the doors and open it."

Cooper looked and indeed saw three doors. They were all identical in shape, but the one on her left was painted blue, the middle one was painted brown, and the one on her right was painted dark green. She looked at them for a moment. Where did they lead? Were there a right one and two wrong ones? Were they all equally good? She had no idea. She knew that Jane was waiting for her answer so that she could continue.

"I choose the door on the left," Cooper said.

"Open the door and enter," said Jane.

Cooper went to the blue door and pulled the handle. As it swung open the other two doors disappeared into the trunk of the tree and only the blue one remained. Cooper peered inside and saw a stone staircase leading down.

"You have chosen the door to the realm of the world below," Jane said. "Descend the staircase."

Cooper stepped inside the tree and set her foot on the first stair. As she did the door swung shut behind her and she saw it disappear. There was nothing there but a smooth stone wall. The only place she could go was down. There were no lights, but somewhere below her a soft glow emanated, allowing her to see as she began to go down the stairs.

Like the path she'd followed to the hill, the stairs spiraled down. She followed them, wondering what was awaiting her in the world below. She was surprised at how easily she was able to envision it all. Part of her—the part that heard Jane's voice—was connected to the real world. But another part was very much walking down a flight of stone stairs, feeling the coolness of the rock and watching the mysterious glow grow brighter.

"You reach the bottom of the stairs," Jane said. "Now you are once more on a path. This one leads you through a forest."

Cooper saw the stairs end at another doorway. When she passed through it, she found herself standing on a path. The glow she had seen came from a pale sun shining above her head. How was it possible that a whole other world existed underground like that? She pushed the thought to the back of her mind as she began walking on the path. It led her through some trees and into a forest, and soon she was walking in the shadows of pine and fir trees.

"Follow the path until you come to a clearing," said Jane. "There you will find someone waiting for you."

Cooper walked some more, following the path as it wandered here and there, seemingly without purpose. She had the distinct feeling that she was being watched, but it didn't frighten her. She knew that no harm could come to her, and whatever watched her was part of her journey.

Suddenly the path ended and she found herself stepping into a clearing. In the center of the clearing there was a rock. And sitting on the rock was a girl. When Cooper saw her, she gasped.

"Bird?" she said, not believing what she was seeing.

The girl looked at her and tilted her head. "Hello," she said. "I've been waiting for you."

Cooper didn't know what to say. She hadn't seen Bird since Midsummer Eve, and seeing her now reminded Cooper of how horrible that night had been. It had been Bird whose music had called to Cooper, luring her into the woods. It had been Bird who had introduced her to Spider and the others who had then put her through the terrible ordeal of being chased through the forest, hunted like a wild pig. And it had been Bird who had ultimately helped her escape from the gang of kids who had called themselves faeries.

But that had been real. This was a meditation. Bird shouldn't have been there. But she was, and she looked just as she had that night, clothed in a thin dress, her long black hair hanging in wild tangles.

"I'm supposed to be looking for my totem animal," Cooper said, confused. This was *her* meditation. How had Bird crept into it?

Bird jumped off the rock and ran to Cooper. "I know," she said.

"You know?" Cooper repeated. "What do you mean you know? What's going on?"

Bird smiled. "I helped you then, and I will help you now," she said. "Watch."

As Cooper looked on, Bird held her hands out and closed her eyes. She began to glow with a faint silver light that grew brighter and brighter. Then she seemed to shrink in on herself, her arms shortening.

The light grew so bright that Cooper had to shield her eyes, and when she took her hand away she saw fluttering before her an owl with silver feathers. Its eyes were green like the forest, and it was watching her intently.

"Bird?" Cooper whispered.

The owl flew to the rock and alighted on it. Cooper followed. She stood in front of the rock, looking on in wonder as the bird ruffled its feathers.

"The creatures of Faerie can take many forms," the owl said, its voice sounding just like Bird's.

"Which is your real one?" Cooper asked.

The owl blinked. "That doesn't matter," it said. "What is important is that I am here to help you on your journey."

Cooper sighed. Suddenly her meditation wasn't as much fun as it had seemed at the beginning. She'd been all too happy to put Bird and the events of Midsummer Eve behind her. Now it seemed that they had come back. But what did it mean? Was Bird really a faerie after all? Or was Cooper simply imagining everything?

"Does it matter?" the owl said, looking at her intently.

"What?" Cooper asked.

"Does it matter?" the owl asked. "Whether I am real or not?"

Cooper looked back at the bird. Its big eyes looked like dark moons nestled among the snowy feathers. She thought about its question. Did it matter whether or not what she saw in her meditation was real? And what was real anyway? It was all in her head, right?

"No," she said finally. "I guess it doesn't matter. Is that the right answer?"

"There are no right answers," the owl said.

Cooper sighed. "If this is *my* meditation, how come you're the one who gets to ask all the questions? I thought my animal totem was supposed to be *helpful*."

"Help comes in many forms," the owl responded. "Sometimes that help is in the form of a question. But yes, I am here to help you. I, too, come in many forms. You may not always recognize me. But I am there, with you, as you journey."

Cooper sighed. "You guys never make it easy, do you?" she asked.

The owl said nothing. It ruffled its feathers again and began to preen them with its beak. Cooper watched it for a few minutes, wondering what to do next. Where was Jane's voice? Why wasn't she reading from the book?

"It is time for me to go now," the owl said. "But we will meet again."

It shook its wings, rising off the rock and gliding away into the forest.

"Wait a minute!" Cooper called after it. "Now where are you going? And what am I supposed to do?"

The owl ignored her, disappearing into the shadows.

"Some totem animal," said Cooper, looking around. "It doesn't even tell me where to go."

"Cooper."

Jane's voice cut through the silence of the forest.

"Cooper."

Cooper jolted awake. Jane was standing over her, shaking her.

"What?" Cooper said, a little annoyed.

"I think you were sleeping," Jane said. "I couldn't get you to wake up."

"You stopped talking," countered Cooper. "I was waiting for you to say something."

"I *tried*," said Jane. "But you were really out of it."

Cooper sat up and rubbed her eyes. "That was really weird," she said.

"What was?" asked Jane.

"The meditation," Cooper told her. "I saw this owl."

"Your totem animal is an owl?" Jane asked.

"Apparently," said Cooper. "But it wasn't all that helpful, really."

"It could be worse," Jane said. "It could have been a llama. Or a Teletubby."

Cooper didn't speak for a moment. She was thinking about what she'd seen during her meditation journey. Once again her mind filled with doubts. Was it all just a big daydream, or had she really contacted a guardian from one of the three inner realms? *I guess I'll never really know*, she told herself.

A knock on Jane's door startled Cooper back to the moment. Jane opened the door and her grandfather looked in. Mr. Goldstein was old and frail. He walked with a cane, and he was leaning on it now as he looked into the room.

"Are you girls all right?" he asked in a voice that was more like the sound of wind in the branches of a tree than anything else.

"We're fine, Grandpa," Jane said. "Do you need me for anything?"

Mr. Goldstein shook his head slowly. Then he looked at Cooper, his large round eyes blinking at her behind his glasses. "I was sleeping," he said. "I had a dream. About her."

Jane looked at Cooper. "You had a dream about Cooper?" she asked.

The old man nodded. "I was back there," he said. "During the war. She came to me. She asked for my help."

Cooper looked at Jane with a puzzled expression on her face. Jane looked away. "It's okay, Grandpa," she said. "We're both fine. I'll come out to make dinner in a minute, okay?"

Mr. Goldstein turned and shuffled down the hallway. When he was gone Cooper asked, "What did he mean he was 'back there'?"

"In the camp," Jane said quietly.

"The concentration camp?" Cooper asked.

She'd seen the faded tattoo on Mr. Goldstein's arm, and she knew that he had lived through one of the infamous Nazi death camps. But Jane never spoke about it, and Cooper didn't know how to ask her without seeming nosy.

"Yes," Jane said. "Sometimes he dreams about it."

"And I was in his dream," Cooper said. "Asking him for help."

"He probably fell asleep right afer seeing you come in," said Jane. "I'm sure it doesn't mean anything."

Cooper thought for a moment. She recalled looking into the owl's eyes. Then she thought about looking into Mr. Goldstein's big dark eyes. *I come in many forms.* That's what her totem animal had told her. *Help comes in many forms.*

Cooper looked at Jane. "I think maybe it does mean something," she said.

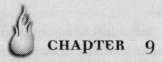

CHAPTER 9

"Something's going on with you."

Annie looked at Eulalie Parsons. The old woman was sitting in the chair beside the window in her room at Shady Hills. Her hands were in her lap and she was watching intently as Annie changed the sheets on the bed.

"Why do you say that?" Annie asked, ducking down to tuck in the corners of the sheet.

Eulalie laughed. "It's all over you," she said simply. "Hanging around like some kind of dog following at your heels."

Annie sighed. She really liked Eulalie, but sometimes it annoyed her that the old woman could tell so much about people just by looking at them. Eulalie said she could see emotions as colors, and she often knew Annie's mood before Annie herself realized why she was feeling a certain way.

"I've just got a lot going on," she said, pulling the bedspread over the sheets. "You know, school and stuff."

"Mmm-hmm," said Eulalie. "And I bet it's the 'stuff' that's got you all worked up."

Annie put her hands on her hips. "I'm *fine*," she said. "Really."

Eulalie pursed her lips but didn't say anything. She just looked at Annie with a steady gaze. Annie looked right back at her, daring her to say something else. After a minute Annie said, "I've got to go do the other rooms. I'll be back later."

She turned and started to walk out, the dirty sheets in her arms. As she was leaving Eulalie said quietly, "Ben doesn't think you're fine either."

Annie stopped. Ben Rowe was the former resident of Eulalie's room. Annie had met him on her very first day as a volunteer at the nursing home. He'd become a good friend to her, and his sudden death over the summer had been hard on her. When Eulalie moved in and Annie discovered that the old woman could talk to Ben's spirit, it had made her feel as if she were still connected to him. Now, though, it just irritated her.

"Tell Ben he worries too much," she said shortly, and walked out.

She threw the sheets from Eulalie's bed into the big wheeled hamper she used on her rounds and began to push it down the hall. *Great*, she thought, *now Ben and Eulalie know that I'm fooling around with my best friend's boyfriend.* The thought upset her. Was it that obvious? What did Eulalie see when she looked at Annie? Annie pictured herself with a big neon sign over her head reading *TRAITOR*. She pictured it flashing on and off, the bright red letters branding her as the horrible person she felt she was.

It had been four days since she and Tyler had made out. Four very long days. She alternated between feeling like she was in a dream and in a nightmare. When she talked to Tyler on the phone—which she'd done every night since their kiss, and when she thought about how it felt to have him hold her, which she did about every three seconds, she was filled with happiness. But when she was with Kate and heard her talking about how much she missed Tyler, or when she thought about how Kate would feel if she knew what had happened between her and Tyler, she wanted to die.

You're overreacting, she scolded herself. *Eulalie and Ben don't know what's going on. They just know that you're upset about something.* She really hoped that was the case. She didn't know what she would do if someone actually asked her if she was getting involved with Tyler. Cooper's grilling at Crones' Circle the week before had been hard enough, and that was before Tyler had even told her that he felt the same way about her that she felt about him. Annie knew that if Cooper asked her now what was going on she would have a really hard time not telling her.

But what is going on? she asked herself. *What are you and Tyler doing?* She stopped pushing the cart and leaned against it. That was the question she couldn't answer. What were the two of them doing? She didn't know, and they hadn't really talked about it. They'd both danced around the issue, almost as if they were pretending that Kate wasn't there—and that, as far as Kate knew, Tyler was still her boyfriend. But they were going to have to talk about these things, and soon. Annie knew that if she had to keep on pretending that nothing was going on she was going to go crazy.

She left the cart where it was and walked down the hall to the pay phone next to the cafeteria. She knew she could use the phone in the nurses' office, but she didn't want anyone to hear what she was saying. She fished in her pocket for change and plunked it into the coin slot. Then she dialed.

"Hello?"

"Hi," Annie said. "It's me."

"Oh, hi," Tyler said happily. "I was just thinking about you."

Annie immediately felt a warm glow inside, but it was quickly extinguished as she thought about why she was calling. "We need to talk," she said.

Tyler was silent on the other end. Then he sighed. "I don't like the sound of that," he said.

"Tyler, we can't ignore what's going on here," Annie told him. "We've got to talk about it."

"I know we do," said Tyler. "And it's not like I haven't been thinking about things."

He paused.

"And what have you been thinking?" asked Annie.

"I've got to tell Kate," said Tyler.

Annie felt her stomach clench into a cold knot of fear. She gripped the receiver tightly and pressed it to her cheek, not saying anything.

"Annie?" Tyler sounded worried.

"I'm here," she said, barely able to talk.

"I think I have to tell her," Tyler repeated. "Don't you?"

Annie took a deep breath. "And what are you going to tell her?" she asked.

Tyler didn't respond. Annie felt her heart pounding as she waited for his answer. When it didn't come, she closed her eyes and leaned her head against the wall. "You don't know, do you?" she said.

"No," admitted Tyler. "I don't know."

"Tyler, what are we doing?" Annie asked, voicing the question she was most afraid of hearing the answer to.

"What do you mean?" he asked.

"You know what I mean," said Annie. "What are we *doing*? Are we just fooling around? Are we going out? What is this? Because, in case you've forgotten, Kate is my best friend and your girlfriend. So I think we should know exactly what we have to tell her."

She sounded angry, and she knew it. But what she felt inside was sadness, an overwhelming sadness that she'd been trying to hold back ever since Tyler had kissed her. She'd tried to convince herself that she was getting what she wanted and that everything would work out. But she couldn't do that anymore.

"This wasn't something I planned, Annie," said Tyler. "It was something that happened. Neither of us meant for it to."

"You sound like you're rehearsing a speech," she said. "You're not answering my question—what are we doing?"

"Maybe I don't know the answer to that!" said Tyler. "It's only been a couple of days since I even let myself feel what I'm feeling."

"But that's what I'm asking you," Annie said. "What are you feeling?"

"Right now?" Tyler said. "Really mixed up. One minute I feel great and the next I feel terrible. And this conversation isn't helping things a whole lot."

"I'm sorry," Annie said. "But I don't like feeling this way either. And I have to see Kate pretty much every day. Do you know what that feels like?"

Tyler sighed. "I know it must be hard," he said.

"Hard?" said Annie. "Try monumentally, terrifyingly, a-billion-times-harder-than-anything-you've-ever-done-hard. That's what it is."

"What do you want me to say?" asked Tyler. "That I'm sorry? I'm sorry you have to go through that. I'm sorry it hurts. I'm sorry that we're in this situation. I'm sorry about a lot of things, Annie, but that doesn't make them go away."

The phone beeped, indicating that it was time

to add more money. Annie reached into her pocket, but she'd used up all of her change. She tried her other pocket, but it, too, was empty.

"We really need to talk this out," Tyler said on the other end. "What is it that *you* want, Annie? What would you tell Kate if you were in my position?"

The phone beeped again. Annie was looking everywhere for more change, but there wasn't any. Before she could give Tyler an answer, the phone went dead.

She slammed the phone down and started to cry. How could things go from good to bad so quickly? Why had she called Tyler and asked him those questions? All she had done was make them both upset. And now he probably thought that she was angry with him. Well, she *was* angry with him. She was also angry with herself. *This isn't like me*, she thought unhappily. *I'm not the kind of person who hurts her best friend.* If someone had told her a month ago that she would be sneaking around with her friend's boyfriend, she would have laughed and said it was crazy. But now she was doing exactly that. And she was smart enough to know that she wouldn't be able to keep it a secret much longer.

She wiped her eyes. Crying about things wasn't going to make them go away. She knew that, too. She had to get back to work. Giving the pay phone a last miserable look, she went back to the laundry hamper and started pushing it again. But her mind kept replaying her conversation with Tyler over and over.

He asked you what you want, she told herself. *What's the answer?* She thought about that as she walked into one of the rooms and began changing the sheets. It was a fair question. What *did* she want from Tyler? Did she want him to be her boyfriend? She supposed she did. After all, isn't that why she'd kissed him? And isn't that why she was so happy when she talked to him? Well, until their last phone call, anyway.

Okay, she thought. *You want him to be your boy-friend.* But was that ever going to happen? Maybe—if he dumped Kate. But then what? Annie would have Tyler, but she would most definitely lose her friend. There was no way Kate would forgive her for some-thing like that. No way. Why had she ever kissed Tyler that first time? Why had she let him know how she felt? She should have just kept all of her feelings inside.

But she hadn't, and now she had to deal with the consequences. She had to make some decisions about what to do next, and no matter what she decided, it wasn't going to be easy. Whatever she decided to do, someone was going to get hurt. And no matter who else got hurt, *she* was going to get hurt.

She finished her rounds, barely noticing what she was doing. Her head was mired in dark thoughts, and she changed the sheets and interacted with the patients as if she were walking in her sleep. By the time the last bed was changed and she'd returned the hamper to the laundry room all she wanted to do was go home.

As she walked to the front doors to leave she passed Eulalie's room. "I thought you were coming back to see me," the old woman said, coming to the doorway.

"I'm kind of tired," Annie told her. "How about next time?"

Eulalie nodded. "Suit yourself," she said. "By the way, I see that dog that's been following you around got a whole lot bigger since I saw him last."

Annie knew this was Eulalie's way of saying that she was ready to listen if Annie was ready to talk. But she wasn't ready. Not yet. As much as what she was going through hurt, she needed to keep it to herself for a while.

"I think I've got him under control," she said, smiling as cheerfully as she could. "But thanks for noticing. And I really will stop by to see you next time I'm in."

"All right, then," said Eulalie. "I'll be seeing you."

She retreated into her room and Annie continued on her way out of the building. When she emerged into the gray November afternoon she was surprised to see Tyler sitting on the steps of the nursing home. She stopped, looking at him.

"I wasn't sure if you hung up on me on purpose or not," he said.

Annie shook her head. "I ran out of change," she said.

Tyler nodded. "That's one less thing to be paranoid about, then," he remarked.

Neither of them spoke for a moment. Annie didn't know whether she should just go home or if she should stay. Part of her wanted to get as far away from Tyler as possible. But she found that she couldn't move.

"I drove," he said finally. "My mother's car. Do you want a ride home?"

Annie nodded. "Okay," she said.

The two of them walked to the car. As Tyler unlocked the door to let Annie in he said, "I know a station wagon isn't exactly cool or anything, but at least it's not a minivan."

Annie got in and Tyler shut the door. Then he let himself in. He started up the car and pulled out of the lot. They drove in silence for a while, Annie looking out the window and Tyler staring straight ahead.

"I've been thinking about what you asked me," Tyler said when they stopped for a red light. "You know, about what we're doing?"

"And?" asked Annie.

"And I think we're making a big mistake," Tyler said.

Annie looked away. She felt a tear slip from her eye and begin to roll down her cheek. She reached up and quickly wiped it away. *Don't let him say anything else*, she pleaded silently. *Please don't let him say anything else.*

The light changed and Tyler continued driving. "I like you, Annie," Tyler said. "I *really* like you. The time we spent together made me see that." He paused. "And it also made me see that maybe Kate and I aren't as perfect a couple as I thought we were."

Annie closed her eyes. She wanted Tyler to stop talking. She didn't want him to say anything that would make her feel worse than she already did. It was like he was tearing the bandage off a wound she had tried hard to cover up, thinking that would heal it. It hurt, and she could feel it deep in her heart.

"If I had never been with Kate, I would do this in a heartbeat," Tyler said.

"But you have been with her, so you can't," said Annie when he didn't continue. She bit her lip. "Do you still love her?" she asked.

"I don't know what I feel right now," Tyler replied. "I honestly don't. I've been away from Kate for so long, and I've been spending so much time with you, that it's hard for me to tell what my real feelings are."

"So we're supposed to wait until you figure out what they are?" asked Annie, looking at him for the first time since they'd started driving.

"Is that asking too much?" Tyler said. "And can you honestly tell me that some of what you're feeling for me isn't about your breakup with Brian?"

Annie started to protest, but stopped. Tyler was right. The two of them had been spending a lot of time together under unusual circumstances. How much of what she felt for him was a result of that? She couldn't honestly say.

Tyler was nearing her neighborhood. "Do you want me to drop you off at your house?" he asked.

"No," Annie said. "I'll get out here."

Neither of them said what they were both thinking—that they didn't want to risk Kate's seeing them together. Although Kate knew that they spent time together, Annie was sure that if she saw either of their faces right at that moment she would know exactly what had been going on.

Tyler pulled over. He turned to face Annie. "I can't deny that I feel something for you," he said. "And part of me wants to take that and just run with it. A big part. But we both have a lot to lose here. You know that."

Annie nodded. "I think maybe we already have lost something," she said. "Neither one of us can take this back."

"I know," Tyler said. "But we don't have to make it any worse. So for now let's just back away."

Annie nodded. She couldn't say anything. She knew that what Tyler was saying was right. In her heart she knew it. But that didn't keep her heart from hurting any less.

Tyler leaned over and kissed her gently. "You're incredibly special," he said.

Annie needed to get out of the car. She couldn't stay any longer. If she did she knew that she would kiss Tyler back, and she didn't want to think about what would happen if she did that.

"I've got to go," she said, opening the door.

She stepped out, not waiting for Tyler's response. The tears were about to come, and she didn't think she could stop them this time. She wanted to get home, where she felt safe. She wanted to lock the door to her room and cry her frustrations out.

The driver's-side door opened and Tyler got out. "Annie," he said. "Don't go like this."

Annie turned away. As she did she looked up and saw Cooper standing in front of her. She was carrying her guitar case. When she saw Annie she smiled. Then she noticed the expression on her friend's face. Then she noticed Tyler standing next to the car.

"Hey, guys," she said, looking from Annie to Tyler. "What's going on here?"

•

CHAPTER 10

"Hey! Where is everybody?"

"Kyle!" Kate ran out of her bedroom and thundered down the stairs. Her big brother was standing in the living room, a duffel bag at his feet. Kate ran up and gave him a huge hug. When she let go she looked up at him.

"What's this?" she asked, indicating the new goatee that covered his chin and upper lip.

"What do you think?" Kyle asked her. "Pretty hot, huh?"

"Oh, very," teased Kate. "If you want to look like a pirate."

Kyle grabbed her and twisted her arm behind her back. Kate squealed and tried to get away, but he was much stronger and he had her trapped. "Say it," Kyle said as he continued to hold her arm.

"It." Kate giggled, earning herself a new round of torment.

"Come on," said Kyle. "I can keep this up all night." He held on even harder.

"Okay!" Kate said. "Okay. You are the supreme lord and master. There, happy?"

"That's better," Kyle said, letting her go. "I'm pleased to see that you remember the magic words."

"I know some other words, too," Kate said, grinning. "Like 'new tattoo.' How about that?"

Kyle narrowed his eyes. "You wouldn't," he said. "I showed you that *only* after you promised never to tell a living soul."

"And I won't," Kate told him. "*If* you help me out with a little problem."

"That's blackmail," Kyle said. Then he nodded. "I like it. So, what am I helping you with?"

"I need to get Mom and Dad to let me start seeing Tyler again," said Kate.

"I didn't know that they'd stopped letting you see him," replied her brother.

"It's a long story," Kate answered.

Kyle looked at his watch. "Dad won't be home for at least a couple of hours," he said. "Where's Mom?"

"Catering a Thanksgiving luncheon for some ladies' club or something," Kate said.

"Then we have time for the sure-to-be-captivating story of your thwarted love," said Kyle as he picked up his bag and walked into the kitchen.

"Fine," said Kate. "But don't eat all the cookies. Mom will skin you."

Kyle, who was at that very moment inspecting the contents of the cookie jar on the counter, responded by taking a handful of freshly baked chocolate chip cookies and popping an entire cookie into his mouth. Then he pulled out a chair and sat down at the table. "Do we have milk?" he asked.

Kate opened the refrigerator and got out the milk. She took a glass from the dish drainer, filled it, and handed it to Kyle. "Who looks after you when you're at school?" she joked.

She poured herself some milk and sat down across from her brother. Then she took one of the cookies from his pile and bit into it. She wasn't sure where to begin the story she wanted to tell Kyle. She'd been going over it in her head for a couple of days, but she still hadn't decided on a final script.

"Spill it already," said Kyle after she had been silent for a minute. "Why did they put the kibosh on your budding romance?"

"They think Tyler is a bad influence on me," Kate told him.

"Tyler?" Kyle said, snorting. "He seems about as bad an influence as—" He searched for a comparison. Finally, he pointed to the milk and cookies in front of him. "As this."

"Probably even less," Kate said.

"Then what happened?" asked Kyle. "Did they catch you two making out on the couch or something?"

Kate shook her head. "No," she said. "In fact, they were really starting to like him."

"Until?" said Kyle.

Kate took a breath. This was the part of the conversation she'd been trying to work out. She was pretty sure that Kyle would be okay with what she had to say next. After all, he was her big brother. He'd looked out for her ever since she was a kid. She knew he wouldn't let her down now.

"Until they found out that he's a witch," she said.

Kyle swallowed the cookie in his mouth. "A witch?" he said. Then he laughed. "What are you talking about?"

"Tyler is Wiccan," said Kate. "He's a witch. So are his mother and sister."

Kyle leaned forward. "You're serious?" he said incredulously.

Kate nodded her response.

"But he's a guy!" Kyle said. "Guys aren't witches."

"What do you think those people who did the ritual for Aunt Netty were?" asked Kate. "They were witches. And some of them were guys."

"Tyler is part of that group?" asked her brother.

"Yes," Kate said. "I asked him not to come that night because I wasn't sure how to tell Mom and Dad. They were already freaked out that Annie and Cooper knew those people. When they found out that I know them, too, they just about lost it."

"What do you mean that you know them, too?" Kyle said. "I thought you told me that you had never met them before."

"I know," Kate said. "I did tell you that. That was

because I didn't know how to tell you about them, and about me."

"What about you?" Kyle asked.

"I'm involved in Wicca, too," said Kate.

Kyle put his glass of milk down. "Come again?"

"I said I'm involved in Wicca, too," repeated Kate, feeling uncomfortable all of a sudden. Kyle was looking at her with an odd expression on his face.

"Are you telling me you think you're a witch?" he asked her.

"No," Kate said. "I'm just part of a study group, that's all." She knew that it wasn't all, but she had realized that Kyle wasn't ready to hear the part about how after her year and a day of study she would probably be initiated as a witch.

Kyle shook his head. "No wonder Mom and Dad said no way to witch boy," he said.

"What do you mean?" asked Kate.

Kyle raised his eyebrows. "Well, clearly you wouldn't be doing this if it wasn't for Tyler. I mean come on, Kate. You, a witch?"

He laughed. Kate was hurt. She hadn't really expected Kyle to understand everything she was telling him, but she certainly hadn't expected him to react so disdainfully. He was treating her news as if it were some kind of joke.

"Kyle, this is really important to me," she said. "I've gone through a lot to get Mom and Dad to understand that. For crying out loud, they even sent me to a shrink."

"And I don't blame them," Kyle retorted. "Kate, I'm sorry they're not letting you see Tyler," he said. "But I can't say that I blame them. The guy may be nice, but if he thinks he's a witch he's not entirely there upstairs, you know?"

"What would you know about it?" snapped Kate. "How many Wiccans do you even know?"

"A few," Kyle said. "There's a group of them at school. They hold these monthly rituals and they're always protesting something or trying to save the trees or whatever. They're freaky. One of them is in my American Lit class. She wears black all the time and doesn't shave her legs."

"No!" Kate said, feigning shock. "Hairy legs? Burn her at the stake!"

"Laugh if you want to," Kyle said. "I'm just saying they're freaky."

"Well, you've met Tyler," replied Kate. "Is he freaky?"

"If he thinks he's a witch, he is," Kyle answered.

"You didn't know that before," argued Kate. "Did you think he was freaky before that?"

"No," Kyle admitted. "But I didn't think that sportscaster on channel seven was freaky, either, until they found the bodies in his cellar."

"Tyler didn't kill anyone," said Kate exasperatedly. "He just practices a religion that you don't understand."

"Religion," scoffed Kyle.

"Look," Kate said, "I'd really love to sit here and

educate you about Wicca, but I really don't have time. Are you going to help me or not?"

Kyle looked at his sister. "You know I love you," he said. "And normally I'd be all over any attempt at overruling Mom and Dad. But I have to tell you, Kate, I think I agree with them about this one."

Kate's heart sank. She'd been counting on Kyle's help. It hadn't even occurred to her that he might side with her parents. She'd expected there to be some misunderstandings on his part, but his total refusal to take Wicca seriously was something she hadn't counted on. All she could do was stare at him.

"I'm sorry," he said, noting her expression.

"Not as sorry as I am," said Kate, getting up and walking out of the kitchen.

"Where are you going?" Kyle called after her.

"Out," said Kate. "Tell Mom I'll be home after class. And no, I don't need a ride. I'll just take my broom."

She snatched her jacket from the hook by the front door and left, pulling it on as she stormed down the sidewalk. Her anger was bubbling over, and she wanted to get away from Kyle before she said something she might regret later. She really did love her brother, and she understood that he didn't know what Wicca was really about. But he'd hurt her, both by mocking her involvement in witchcraft and by acting as if he was older and wiser than she was and therefore knew what was best for her.

She caught the bus going downtown and arrived

at Crones' Circle well before the start of class. She walked in and was surprised and delighted to see Tyler there. When he saw her come in, he walked over to her.

"What are you doing here?" he asked.

"It's nice to see you, too," said Kate, taken aback by his tone of voice.

"That's not what I mean," said Tyler. "I meant class doesn't start for another hour."

"Were you timing your visit so you would miss me or something?" joked Kate.

Tyler laughed. "Why would I do that?" he asked. "I just came to bring Sophia something from my mother."

"Then fate brought us together," Kate said. "Although who knew fate looked like my big, stupid bear of a brother?"

"Your brother?" Tyler said. "What does he have to do with anything?"

Kate sighed. "I was trying to enlist his help in loosening my parents up about us," she explained. "I thought with him here for the holiday and all we could get my parents to change their minds about our seeing one another."

"I see," Tyler said. "And he didn't like this idea?"

Kate shook her head. "He wasn't wild about it," she said. "So I left and came here. I needed to be around people who actually know something about Wicca. I'm tired of being the only pagan in the family." She smiled. "Plus, I got to see you."

She leaned up and kissed Tyler. When she pulled away she looked at him curiously. "Is something wrong?" she asked.

"No," Tyler said. "Why?"

"Because you seemed about as excited by that kiss as you would be if Simeon kissed you," said Kate, nodding at the big gray cat who was the mascot of Crones' Circle and who was sleeping on the counter behind them.

"I'm *very* excited about seeing you," Tyler said.

"Okay," said Kate doubtfully.

"But I have to go," continued Tyler. "I'm late. I'm sorry."

Kate groaned. "Our weekly ten minutes and you're cutting it short by five," she remarked.

"I'm really sorry," Tyler told her. "But my mother is expecting me home. We'll talk soon, okay?"

"Yeah," Kate said. "I'll write you letters and have Annie smuggle them to you."

"I've *really* got to go now," Tyler said. He picked up a bag that was sitting on the counter and gave her a quick kiss on the cheek. "Bye."

He left the store, walking quickly. Kate, watching him go, said, "Bye. I love you." But the door had already shut and Tyler was gone.

"Aaaaahhhhhh," Kate said. "This sucks!"

"Bad day?" asked Sophia, appearing from the rear of the store. She was carrying a small box, which she set on the counter and opened with a small knife.

"That would be one way to describe it," answered Kate.

Sophia pulled some packing paper out of the box, then reached in and pulled out some decks of Tarot cards. "Anything I can do to help?" she asked.

"Not unless you have a spell for making my brother less pigheaded," Kate told her.

"Can't help you there," said Sophia, removing more cards. "But how about a spell for working out problems?"

"Does it work?" asked Kate.

"You know better than to ask me that," Sophia said. "It works if you put the right energy into it." She reached into a drawer beneath the counter and pulled out a length of string. She held it up. "This is your problem," she said.

"And what do I do with it?" Kate asked.

"Cast your circle," Sophia explained. "Sit in it and do your favorite energy-raising activity. When you're feeling all charged up, hold the string in your hands."

Sophia stretched the string between her two hands. "Think about the things that are bothering you," she said, bringing the ends together. "For each one, tie a knot in the string. When you've got all your problems tied up, hold the string in your hands and feel the energy filling it."

She tied several knots in the string and held it up. "Now for the good part. When you feel ready, untie the knots you made and imagine all of the energy being released. That energy is the energy you're wasting right now by worrying about those problems. When you untie the knot you're freeing that energy for other purposes. You're undoing the problem and letting the universe handle it for you."

She untied the knots as she spoke. When she was done she wiggled the string at Kate. "There's *knot*-thing to it," she said.

Kate groaned. "Stick with the magic," she said. "Comedy is definitely *knot* your thing."

"Try it," said Sophia.

"I will," Kate told her. "Although I'm going to have some pretty big knots." She thought about the things she was having trouble with. Her parents. Kyle. And now Tyler. He wasn't a problem, really, but he was definitely acting strangely.

"How was the ritual over at Botanica Yemaya the other night?" asked Sophia.

"Intense," Kate replied. "One of the orishas talked to me."

"I've heard about that happening," said Sophia.

"You've never been to one of those things?" Kate asked, surprised. She'd assumed that Sophia would know about all things pagan.

"They almost never invite outsiders," said Sophia. "You were very lucky. What did the orisha say to you?"

"He said that I was one of his children," Kate said. "And he blew smoke in my face. It was sort of weird. I mean, I'm not even Santerian."

"You're not Asatru or Native American or Mayan, either," Sophia said. "But you've worked with deities from all of those cultures. Wicca doesn't have any one god or goddess who belongs only to us. We draw from many different traditions—sharing them, if you will. There's no reason why this orisha wouldn't come to you."

"But what am I supposed to do about it?" Kate asked.

"Talk to Evelyn," said Sophia. "She can tell you better than I can. I'm sure she'd be happy to see you again."

The bell over the door tinkled and Kate turned to see Cooper and Annie coming in. She waved at her friends. "Hey," she said. "I got here early. You guys missed Tyler."

"Oh," said Annie.

"Look," Cooper said. "New Tarot cards!"

She and Annie began to look through the new decks, inspecting them with great interest. Kate watched them for a moment. *Why are they acting all weird, too?* she wondered. *First Tyler and now Annie and Cooper.* They were all acting strangely. *It must be the holidays,* she told herself. *They always stress people out.*

Annie caught her eye and gave her a big smile. Kate smiled back. *If this keeps up,* she thought, *by Christmas we'll all be totally nuts.*

CHAPTER 11

"How are the potatoes?"

Cooper poked at the pile on her plate, spearing a lump. She picked it up and examined it, then put it down. "They're good," she said.

"I got the recipe out of *Martha Stewart Living*," said her mother.

"The dressing is good, too," Mr. Rivers told her.

"There are oysters in it," explained Cooper's mother.

The three of them settled into a morose silence as they ate. As Cooper chewed on a bite of squash she stared at the platter of turkey sitting in the center of the table. Her father had carved the bird up and it sat there in pieces, the two legs on either side of a mound of bits and pieces that used to be its body. Thinking of having to eat it, Cooper was glad that she had declared herself a vegetarian years before.

Not that these vegetables are much better, she thought grimly. *She might have gotten the recipe from Martha*

Stewart Living, *but they taste more like something out of* Arts & Crafts Monthly's *Fun with Paste! issue*.

Thanksgiving wasn't until the next day, but Mrs. Rivers had decided to hold the event the night before because Mr. Rivers was going out of town on business. She'd also, in a move that had completely shocked both Cooper and her father, decided to cook the dinner herself. Since her mother was known more for how well she ordered in than how well she worked a stove, Cooper had been doubtful about her ability to pull a complete Thanksgiving spread off. And she'd been right. While the food was edible, it wasn't particularly good. Mrs. Rivers was attempting to make the best of it, but Cooper could tell that her mother's false enthusiasm was failing.

"More green beans, anyone?" Mrs. Rivers asked.

"Not for me," Mr. Rivers answered, pulling what looked like a twig out of his mouth and laying it on his plate. "But the cranberry sauce is great."

"It came out of a can," Mrs. Rivers said dully.

Cooper's father looked at her and raised his eyebrows helplessly. Cooper knew that he wanted her assistance in trying to salvage what they could of the tense get-together.

"You did a great job, Mom," she said brightly.

Mrs. Rivers looked at her. "No," she said. "I didn't. We all know it, so you two don't have to pretend just to spare my feelings. I'm a big girl. I can take it."

"It doesn't matter, Janet," Mr. Rivers said.

"Not to you, Stephen," said Mrs. Rivers. "But you aren't the only one here."

Cooper's father put down his fork. He sighed and rubbed his forehead. "I knew we should have gone out," he said.

Cooper looked at her parents. She knew that things were about to turn ugly. Ever since her father had arrived at the house, her parents had been on edge with one another. It was the first time they'd spent more than an hour together, and Cooper could tell that with each passing minute things were growing more and more tense.

She tried to ignore what was going on and think of something else, but the only other thing that came to mind was Annie and Tyler. Ever since running into them on Monday, she'd been trying to figure out exactly what was going on with her friends. She hadn't been surprised to see them together, but she *had* been surprised to see Annie on the verge of tears. And when she'd found out *why* Annie had been about to cry, she'd been so floored that she couldn't say anything.

Annie and Tyler. Cooper almost laughed, the idea of it was so funny. Tyler was the perfect guy— the understanding and sensitive boyfriend. And Annie, Annie was the good girl who never did anything to hurt anyone. The idea of the two of them together when Tyler was supposed to be in love with Kate was so far from believable that it sounded like a science fiction story. But the fact that they really *were* wasn't funny.

It had taken Annie a little while to tell Cooper everything. But she had told her, while sitting in her bedroom, and afterward Cooper had been unable to say anything coherent. She'd been convinced that it was a joke. But Annie's tear-stained face was no joke, and Cooper had finally done the only thing she could—she'd held Annie while her friend cried over her broken heart.

Cooper felt bad for Annie. But she felt almost worse for Kate, who had no idea that her best friend and her supposed boyfriend were doing more than just going to the movies together. Cooper had agreed not to say anything to Kate and let Annie and Tyler decide what to do about it, but she still wasn't sure if that was the right decision. True, Annie and Tyler had called it off. But where did that leave things? They had still betrayed Kate, and that was bound to change things between them all, even if they *never* told her about it.

"Why do you always have to say 'I told you so?'" Mrs. Rivers's accusation cut through Cooper's daydreams and brought her back to the moment.

"I didn't say 'I told you so,'" said Mr. Rivers defensively.

"This isn't a courtroom, Stephen," Cooper's mother countered. "You don't have to win every argument the way you win cases."

"This isn't an argument," said Cooper's father.

"Don't speak to me like I'm a five-year-old child," Mrs. Rivers said, glaring at him.

"Are you guys going to do this for much longer?" asked Cooper. "Because I could really use some pumpkin pie."

Her parents looked at her in surprise.

"No, really," Cooper said tiredly. "If you're just going to fight I might as well just eat pie in my room, because this isn't a whole lot of fun. Unless you guys are having fun, that is."

Her mother and father looked at one another. Her mother put down her fork and cleared her throat. "I'm sorry, Cooper," she said. "I wanted this to be a nice time." She glared at her husband.

"*I* wanted this to be a nice time, too," said Mr. Rivers. He began to say something else but shut his mouth. Then he looked at Cooper. "Cooper, we weren't going to discuss this until later, but your mother and I have decided that we're going to separate permanently."

"You mean divorce?" Cooper said. "Isn't that what 'separate permanently' means?"

No one said anything for a moment. Then her mother said, "Yes, that's what it means."

Cooper looked at her plate. She couldn't look at her parents. Divorced. Her parents were getting divorced.

"But it's only been a couple of months since you separated," said Cooper, as if that made any difference.

"We know you were hoping for a different out-come," said her mother. "We were, too."

"Then why did we get this one?" asked Cooper.

"Sometimes things can't work out the way that would make things easiest," Mr. Rivers replied.

"So now that I'm going to be the product of a broken home, how is it going to work?" Cooper said.

"You and your mother will continue to live here," said her father. "I'm going to be getting my own place."

"Great," said Cooper. "Now I'll have *two* places to call home. And when you guys get remarried maybe I'll have a whole bunch of wicked stepsisters and stepbrothers to hang out with."

"No one is getting remarried," said Mrs. Rivers.

"Why not?" Cooper said. "What's the point of splitting up if not to find better options?"

She knew she was being cruel, but she couldn't help herself. She was angry, and she was taking her frustration out on her parents because they happened to be sitting across from her. Plus, she blamed them for letting this happen. She knew that wasn't a reasonable thing to think, but she thought it nonetheless. While the mature part of her brain knew full well that sometimes people's lives took them in different directions, the part of her that was still six years old wanted to have her mommy and daddy back together. It was that part that had taken over control of her mouth at the moment.

"I'll be up in my room," she said, pushing back from the table. "Let me know when the visitation schedule is all drawn up."

She stormed out of the room and up the stairs, making sure her boots made scuffs on the polished wood surfaces. Then she went into her room and slammed the door. She knew they wouldn't come after her. Not yet. And she didn't want them to. She didn't want to hear about how they both still loved her, or about how the situation had nothing to do with her. She didn't want to hear about how this would be best for everyone, even if it was hard. Those things might be true, but they didn't make her feel better.

What is it with people? she thought angrily. *Why can't they manage not to screw things up?* Her parents had seemed to have a good relationship, but now they were telling her that it was over. Annie and Tyler were doing whatever it was they were doing. Everybody seemed determined to ruin what they had.

Are T.J. and I next? she asked herself. *Why should we be any different? Why should we stay together? What's the point?*

She needed to get out of the house. She couldn't stay there just stewing and waiting for her parents to come up for a lame talk that would only make her more upset. She needed to get away from them, at least for a while.

She grabbed her keys from the dresser and left

her room. Being as quiet as she could, she went downstairs and out the front door, pulling it shut behind her. Then she walked quickly to her car, got in, and drove away before her parents could come out and try to stop her.

She drove around aimlessly for a while, not really caring where she went. She just liked driving. She liked being inside her car with the blackness surrounding her, the headlights cutting through the dark like a cat's eyes. She liked hearing the hum of the engine, and the way it made her feel like she was flying. She didn't even turn on the radio. She didn't want the distraction.

Driving was almost like meditating, she decided. It calmed her and made her feel both more relaxed and more powerful. As she drove she felt the anger and hurt inside of her slipping away, left behind on the road as she sped into the night.

She decided to drive to Jane's house. The way she was feeling, she didn't really want to see T.J. That would only remind her of what had upset her in the first place. And she didn't want to see Annie or Kate, for the same reason. But she could talk to Jane. And she found that she wanted to talk.

She pulled up in front of the Goldstein house and parked. Turning the lights off, she got out and walked to the front door. She rang the buzzer and waited for Jane to let her in.

But when the door opened, it wasn't Jane's face looking out at her. It was her grandfather's. Mr.

Goldstein blinked in the harsh glare of the porch light.

"Jane isn't here," he said when he saw Cooper. "She's out."

"Oh," Cooper said. It hadn't occurred to her that Jane might be doing something else, and she felt foolish for not having called first to check. "I'm sorry for bothering you, Mr. Goldstein. Could you please tell Jane that I'll call her later?"

Cooper started to walk away.

"Wait," said Mr. Goldstein in his thin voice. "Come back. I want to talk to you."

Cooper turned around and looked at the old man. He was beckoning to her with one thin finger. "Come inside," he said.

Cooper did as he asked, not really because she wanted to but because she was so surprised that Mr. Goldstein had spoken so many words at once. He was generally so quiet, and she was curious to see what had made him call afer her.

Mr. Goldstein shut the door and began walking down the hallway, motioning for Cooper to follow him. He walked into the living room, where he slowly lowered himself into the big armchair that Cooper usually saw him in. Generally he was staring at the TV or half heartedly reading a book or a magazine, but now his eyes were alert and clear as he motioned for Cooper to sit down in the room's other chair.

She sat and waited for him to speak. He continued

to look at her quizzically for a few minutes, and Cooper almost thought that perhaps he'd fallen asleep with his eyes open. But then he blinked, startling her, and spoke.

"I dreamed of you again," he said simply.

Cooper waited for more, but nothing came. She cleared her throat. "You mean the dream about being in—" She couldn't finish the sentence. She didn't want to upset Jane's grandfather by talking about what surely must be a horrible memory.

"In the camp," Mr. Goldstein said, nodding. "Yes."

Cooper nodded while Mr. Goldstein took a deep breath. "My granddaughter does not like me to talk about the camp," he said. "She thinks it makes me sad." He paused thoughtfully. "And it does. But it also makes me happy."

"Happy?" Cooper repeated, not sure she had heard correctly. Mr. Goldstein's voice was very soft, and it was easy to miss what he said unless she was paying close attention.

"Yes," he said. "It makes me happy. Perhaps that is not quite the right word. I'm old. I don't remember things all the time. But you know what I mean."

"No," Cooper said. "Actually, I don't know."

Mr. Goldstein sighed. "Those who were not there cannot really understand," he said. "There was horror in the camps. There was much horror. What was done to people broke my heart. Seeing my friends and family murdered—that was enough to make me doubt the existence of God."

The old man looked down for a moment, as if remembering a particularly difficult memory. Then he looked up at Cooper. "But there was much love there, too. The love of fathers for sons, and sisters for brothers. The love of friends for friends and husbands for wives. Even in the middle of hell, we still loved one another. Even when they tore us from one another's arms, they could not take away the love we had for one another in our hearts. And that's how some of us survived."

Cooper sat silently, listening. She didn't know what had made Mr. Goldstein want to tell her the things he was saying, but she figured he had a reason. For the moment all she could do was sit and listen to him talk.

"In my dream," he said, "you came to me in the camp. Your face was dirty. Your clothes were torn. You were thin, and frightened."

Cooper felt a peculiar chill begin to wrap its arms around her. As Mr. Goldstein spoke she pictured in her mind the things he was speaking of. She saw herself wearing an old tattered dress, too thin to keep out the cold, and shoes that were too small for her feet. She wondered how she could have such a vivid memory of something that had never actually happened to her, but she did. It was almost as if she were watching a movie of something that had happened before she was old enough to really remember it.

"You see it," Mr. Goldstein said. "You remember. You came to me, and you asked me to help you find a way out."

Cooper looked at the old man and saw that tears had started to fall from his eyes. "But I couldn't help you," he said. "I couldn't remember the way out. And they came and took you."

"The soldiers," Cooper whispered.

Mr. Goldstein nodded. Then he leaned forward and grabbed her hands. "I could not help you then," he said. "But I can now. Look for the love. It is the way out. It will save you."

Cooper looked into his eyes. For a moment she thought she saw herself reflected in them—herself with shorn hair and a dirty face. But then the image was gone, and she was looking at Mr. Goldstein's wrinkled face while he repeated over and over, "Look for the love, little one. Look for the love."

He sounds like an owl, Cooper thought suddenly. *Repeating the same thing over and over*. The idea struck her as odd. Then she remembered—the owl. Once before she had looked at Mr. Goldstein and thought that he looked like an owl. And she had wondered if maybe, like Bird in her vision quest, he had been sent to give her a clue of some kind. Now, as she sat holding his hands and listening to him whispering to her, she knew that was true. She looked down and saw that where the sleeve of his sweater had pulled back, the faded tattoo on his arm was showing. She ran her finger over it lightly. He *had* given her something she could use. He had given her hope. Yes, maybe things were falling apart around her. But that didn't mean everything was hopeless. She still had love to cling to—her love for her mother and father, her love for her friends, and her love for T.J. Even if the relationships between them were strained, she still had her love for them. That was what would keep her going.

"Thank you," she said to Mr. Goldstein.

"I'm sorry I could not help you in my dream," he said. "But perhaps I have now, eh?"

"Yes," Cooper said. "Yes, you have."

"Then it is good," said the old man.

"It's more than good," said Cooper, giving his hands a final squeeze and then letting go. She stood up. "Tell Jane I'll call her later," she said. "There's something I have to go do."

Mr. Goldstein waved her out of the room kindly. "You know the way out," he said.

Cooper left the house and got into the car. She pulled away and drove into the darkness. But this time she knew exactly where she was going—home. She had some things to say to her parents. *And then*, she thought, *then I might just call T.J.*

CHAPTER 12

Becka and Annie raced up the stairs and into Annie's room, shutting the door behind them. Becka dropped her bag on the floor and looked around.

"Very cool," she said. "I love it. You have privacy *and* your own bathroom."

"I know," Annie said. "It's pretty much perfect."

Becka was walking around the room looking at everything. She stopped in front of the big painting that hung on the wall opposite Annie's bed. "Did your mom do this?" she asked.

Annie nodded. "That's her holding me."

"I love the way the moon looks like it has a face," said Becka.

She sees it, Annie thought happily to herself. Not everyone who looked at the painting noticed that it had the features of a woman's face. The Goddess, as Annie liked to think of her. She liked that Becka had seen it right away.

Becka turned around. "This feels a little weird," she said. "I mean, I live in your old house in San

Francisco and now I'm visiting your new house here. I feel like I should be giving you something of mine. Which reminds me," she added, kneeling and unzipping her bag, "I brought you something." She pulled a package out of the bag and handed it to Annie.

Annie looked at the package, which was wrapped in bright pink paper, and hefted it in her hand. "What is it?" she asked Becka.

"A little something from me and Dixie," said Becka. "To remind you of San Francisco."

"Like I could ever forget," joked Annie as she tore the paper off. Inside was a T-shirt. It, too, was pink. Annie held it up and saw that across the front was written BECAUSE I'M THE QUEEN, THAT'S WHY.

"Dixie wanted it for himself," said Becka. "But I insisted that it would look much better on you."

"I love it," Annie told her. "Thanks."

"So, what's on the agenda for the weekend?" Becka asked, sitting on the end of Annie's bed.

"Well, tomorrow we slave away in the kitchen all day, consume massive quantities of food, watch giant balloons shaped like cartoon characters get dragged down a New York street, and then fall into a stupor. But tonight is wide open. Is there anything you want to do?"

"It would be fun to meet your friends," said Becka. "You've told me so much about them that I feel like I know them already."

"That could be a problem," said Annie hesitantly.

"Why?" Becka asked when Annie didn't continue. "Don't you think they'd like me?"

"Oh, no!" replied Annie. "I think they'd *love* you. It's just that Cooper is having an early Thanksgiving with her folks and Kate—" She stopped.

"Is in a women's prison?" Becka said dramatically. "What?"

Annie sighed. "Can I talk to you about something?" she asked.

"Sure," Becka said. "I'm all ears."

"It doesn't make me look very good," said Annie warily. "To tell the truth, I'm terrified that you'll think I'm a horrible person."

"It must be *really* good, then," Becka replied. Then, seeing Annie's face, she said, "Seriously, I don't think I could ever think of you as a bad person. So spill it."

Annie sat down on the bed. She badly wanted to tell Becka what she was going through. She needed to talk to someone who wasn't as close to the situation as Cooper was, and definitely not as close as Kate was. Although she and Becka really only knew one another from their telephone calls, Annie felt that they were friends. At least, she hoped they were.

Still, she didn't know how to say what she had to say. No matter what form it took, it sounded awful to her. Finally she just took a deep breath and said quickly, "I sort of cheated on Kate with her boyfriend. Well, as much as you can cheat on someone you're not actually romantically involved with. But you get the idea."

Becka's eyes went wide. She opened her mouth. Then she closed it again. Then she opened it again.

"You look like a fish," Annie said.

Becka did the opening-and-closing-her-mouth thing a few more times. "Um—wow," she said finally.

"You *do* think I'm a horrible person," Annie said.

Becka shook her head. "No, I don't," she said. She looked at Annie for a moment. "When you say you cheated, do you mean that you—you know?" She raised her eyebrows and waited for Annie's answer.

Annie looked at her for a moment, confused. Then she realized what Becka was asking. "Oh!" she said, a little shocked. "No. I mean, I've never. No, we didn't. No. Definitely not."

Becka smiled slightly. "Then what exactly do you mean?" she asked.

"We kissed," Annie said. "But that wasn't the big deal, really. It was more the way we felt about each other."

"Meaning?" Becka queried.

Annie bit her lip for a moment. How could she best explain what had gone on between her and Tyler? "It was like we both felt that if the situation was different, the two of us would be together," she said.

Becka nodded. "Got you," she said. "If Kate wasn't around, you'd be the one smooching with him."

"It's like we're just more right together than he and Kate are," Annie said, talking to herself as much as to Becka.

"But not enough for him to break up with her?" asked Becka.

"I don't know what he'll do," said Annie. "But even if he did do that, we couldn't be together. That would just be too weird. I mean, Kate's my best friend. We've been through a lot together."

"And now the problem is that you feel weird around her," Becka said. "Because you feel all guilty."

"Right," Annie said. "Even though nothing is going on between me and Tyler right now, every time I see Kate's face I think about how she trusts me and how I betrayed that trust. I want to tell her everything and just get it out in the open."

"Don't!" Becka exclaimed. "Whatever you do, do *not* tell her about this."

"But—" Annie began.

Becka reached out and touched her leg. "Just listen," she said. "I know how you feel. Trust me, I do. And I can tell you that the absolute worst thing you can do is tell Kate about this. The only person who will feel any better is *you*. You want to tell her because you want to get it off your chest. You want her to forgive you. But you know what? She's going to feel horrible, because you're going to put her in this position where if she doesn't forgive you she looks like the bad guy, and if she says she forgives you when she doesn't she's going to hurt like crazy. Right now she doesn't know anything about this. You and Tyler seem to have decided that things between you aren't going to go anywhere. Maybe he'll break up with Kate. Maybe he won't. But this is about you and Kate."

Becka stopped talking and took Annie's hand. "I know that was a long speech," she said. "But this is something I know about. Someone cheated on me once. He decided to come clean, and I really wish he hadn't. It wasn't going to happen again, and it didn't mean anything. It was just something that happened. But as soon as I found out, it made me doubt everything. I ended up losing a great guy and a great friend because I couldn't handle it."

"But if I don't tell her, then I'm always going to feel guilty," Annie said.

"Maybe you will," answered Becka. "Maybe it will go away with time. But look at it as the price you have to pay to make your friend happy by keeping her in the dark. You made a mistake, Annie. We all make mistakes. Don't make it worse now by dumping your hurt on Kate so that you can try to feel better. Tell me. Tell Cooper. Tell whoever you know will listen and keep their mouth shut. But there's one person you never tell, and that's Kate."

Annie felt the tears beginning to come. She

sniffled, holding them back. "I was so stupid," she said. "All I had to do was not kiss him. Why couldn't I do that? Of all the guys in the world, why did I have to go and kiss *that* one?"

"Because you did," said Becka. "Don't analyze it. Beat yourself up a little bit and then let it go."

"I don't know how," Annie told her. "I just don't know how."

Becka looked at her thoughtfully. "How about a little ritual?" she suggested. "You know how you and Dixie did that one to help your parents? Well, do one to get rid of what you're feeling. Can you do something like that?"

Annie thought about the suggestion for a minute. "Maybe I could," she thought. She looked at Becka. "Do you want to help me?"

"Me?" Becka said. "What can I do?"

"The same thing you did when we did the ritual in my old house," said Annie. "You can lend your energy."

"Sure," Becka said. "If you think it will help."

"It can't hurt," Annie said.

She went to her closet and got five white candles. She placed four of them on the floor at the points where the four directions would be on a circle, and the fifth one she placed in the center of the circle. Then she looked around the room.

"I'll be right back," she told Becka.

She left and went downstairs. A few minutes later she returned carrying something in her hand.

"What is that?" Becka asked.

Annie held up a small round stone. "I got it out of the garden," she said. "I'm sure they're all down there wondering what we're up to."

Becka giggled. "What are *they* doing?"

"Aunt Sarah and your dad are making pasta sauce," Annie told her. "She was feeding it to him from the spoon."

Becka laughed again. "I hope she's a better cook than he is then," she said. "He couldn't boil water."

"Then we're in trouble," said Annie. "We'll go down and rescue them from themselves when we're done here. But let's get this going."

"What are we going to do with the rock?" Becka asked.

"You'll see in a minute," Annie replied. "Right now let's cast the circle."

She had Becka sit on one side of the central candle and she sat on the other. She took matches and lit the first candle. "Flame of the East," she said. "Spirit of air. Burn brightly in our circle." Then she lit the second, saying, "Flame of the South, spirit of fire. Burn brightly in our circle." The third and fourth candles, symbolizing the flames of the North and the West, were then lit with similar incantations invoking the spirits of water and earth. Then Annie lit the central candle. As she did she said, "Flame of the center, spirit of healing. Burn brightly in our circle."

When she was finished lighting the candles she

looked across the flame at Becka. "Do you remember how we raised energy the last time?" she asked her. "We visualized white light coming up from the earth and out through our hands."

"Right," Becka said.

"We're going to do something like that now," Annie told her. "The purpose is the same. We want our intentions to empower the circle. We want the energy to fill the sacred space. But there are many ways of doing that. The white light of meditation is just easiest for most people, which is why we did it that way before."

"How will we do it this time?" Becka asked her.

"I want to try something," Annie replied. "I've been reading about the Asatru practices. Asatru is the religion of the Norse people," she added when Becka looked at her blankly.

Becka nodded. "I don't really know about that," she said.

"They were really into the idea of there being balance in nature," said Annie. "Dark and light, birth and death, the sun and the moon. That sort of thing. The ritual we're doing is all about balance, in a way. So maybe we can try raising energy by saying words that balance each other. Cooper and Kate and I have done something similar before where we go around the circle each saying a word that reminds us of the word said by the previous person."

"So you'll say a word and I'll say a word that I think balances it?" Becka said.

Annie nodded. "Close your eyes," she said. "As we say the words, imagine the circle glowing with two kinds of energy. One can be golden. Imagine it swirling clockwise around the circle, surrounding us. The other can be purple. Imagine it swirling counterclockwise, or widdershins."

"Good word," Becka remarked.

"It sounds so much better than *counterclockwise*," Annie agreed. "Anyway, imagine the purple energy flowing widdershins. The two of them balance one another. Ready?"

"Go for it," said Becka.

Annie closed her eyes and let a word appear in her thoughts. "Summer," she said, and immediately pictured a drop of golden light rolling around the circle, forming a boundary.

"Winter," Becka replied, and Annie could see the purple energy flowing in the opposite direction. The two colors passed one another, forming two half circles before completing their rounds and finishing the two separate, but adjoining, circles.

Annie thought of another word. "Joy," she said.

Becka paused a moment, then said, "Sadness."

With each new set of words, Annie felt the two powers that composed the circle growing stronger. It was like holding on to a string and feeling someone pulling on the other end while she pulled on her end. The energies complemented one another, and together they made one circle of power.

They went through a dozen groups of words.

Then Annie stopped. The circle felt strong enough for her. She opened her eyes and saw Becka sitting across from her, eyes closed and with a smile on her lips.

"You can open your eyes," Annie told her.

Becka blinked. "I can feel it," she whispered excitedly. "It's like being in a whirlpool!"

"That was kind of what I was going for," Annie said. She picked up the rock and held it in her hands. "Now for step two. This rock represents how I feel inside—hard and cold. It also represents earth, and the earth can absorb a lot of things and transform them into energy. I'm going to put all of my feelings of sadness and fear into the rock."

"And then what?" Becka asked. "Hurl it through someone's window?"

"No," Annie said, laughing at Becka's suggestion. "I'm going to put it back in the garden."

"Which will achieve what?" Becka asked.

"The garden is a beautiful place," said Annie. "We have a lot of happy times there, and we grow things there. The energy is very positive. I want the negative energy I put into the rock to be changed— to be transformed—by being in that place. But mostly I want to take it out of me so that I can feel more balanced, like the circle."

Becka nodded. Annie clasped her hands around the stone and closed her eyes. "I'm picturing all of the negativity in me pouring into the stone," she informed Becka. "I see it as a kind of sickly green color. I let it flow out of my hands and into the rock."

She sat for a few minutes, letting the feelings of unhappiness inside of her well up and pour into the stone in her hands. When she felt as if the last bit of it was gone from inside of her, she opened her hands and lifted the rock up.

"Touch it," she instructed Becka.

Becka put a finger out and stroked the stone. "It's so cold!" she said. "But you were holding it in your hands. It should be warm."

"Weird, huh?" Annie said. "Now we can go stick it back in the garden. There's a place right by the lavender plants that I think will be perfect."

Becka started to get up but Annie stopped her. "We need to open the circle," she said, and Becka resumed her spot.

"Picture the two energies swirling faster and faster," said Annie. "Imagine them running together like water going down a drain. Picture them both sinking into the ground."

As she told Becka what to do, Annie did the same thing. She saw the purple and the gold energies circling at greater and greater speed, then spiraling down into the ground. When the last of the energy was gone she said, "The circle is open but unbroken."

"We're done?" asked Becka curiously.

"We're done," said Annie.

They stood up and Annie blew out the candles.

Then she picked up the rock. "Let's put this baby outside," she said.

"Wait a minute," said Becka. "You haven't told me if it helped or not."

"I feel better," said Annie. "Whether or not it will last, I don't know. But I feel better."

Becka looked at the rock. "Now, don't *you* go telling anyone what you know about this," she said.

Annie laughed. "Come on," she told Becka. "Let's get down there and see what the two mad chefs have done."

As they left the room Becka paused and remarked, "You know, the more of this Wicca stuff I do, the more I like it."

"Uh-oh," replied Annie. "Now we're *all* in trouble."

CHAPTER 13

"Kate, would you put this on the table?"

Mrs. Morgan handed her daughter a bowl of gravy. Kate took it and plopped it unceremoniously on the table. A little bit of it spilled over the side and splattered on the linen tablecloth. Kate looked at the ugly stain and thought, *That's exactly how I feel*.

Nothing was going right. Cooper and Annie had acted strangely at class on Tuesday night. Tyler had seemed distant. And Kyle was being totally not cool to her. Instead of listening to her and accepting that even though *he* didn't understand it, Wicca was something that was important to her, he had decided to make a joke out of it. He didn't do it in front of their parents, because he was smart enough to know that it would make them angry, but whenever he could he would make little remarks to Kate. The night before, when she'd spilled some milk on the floor in the kitchen, he'd leaned over and said, "Why don't you just wiggle your nose and make it disappear?"

Kate knew that he was being that way because

he didn't understand. But she was angry at him anyway. Kyle had always been her ally against her parents, ever since she was old enough to need someone to take her side. It had been Kyle who had argued successfully for Kate to be able to get her ears pierced. It was Kyle who had convinced Mr. Morgan that Kate should be allowed to go with him to her first rock concert. It was Kyle and Kate—as a team—who had once gotten the family's summer vacation destination changed from the Grand Canyon to Disneyland.

But not now. Kate looked at her brother. He was sitting on the couch, watching TV and eating all the olives out of the dish Kate had placed on the table fifteen minutes earlier. *I wish I was magic*, Kate thought to herself. *I'd turn you into the little rat you are.*

"Kate?"

Kate turned around and saw her mother looking at her. "Did you hear me?" Mrs. Morgan asked. "I asked if the salt and pepper were on the table."

"Oh," Kate said. She scanned the table. "No, they're not. I'll get them."

"Something wrong?" Mrs. Morgan asked as Kate went to the cupboard to find the missing condiments. "You seem angry."

"No," replied Kate, trying to sound fine. "I'm okay."

"You've barely said three words to Kyle since

he got here," Mrs. Morgan said.

"That's because he hasn't stopped eating since he got here," said Kate, rummaging behind the cinnamon and the paprika and seeing the pepper but not the salt. "It's hard to talk to someone whose mouth is always full."

Mrs. Morgan sighed. "In other words, you're mad at him and you're not going to tell me why?"

Kate found the salt but pretended that she hadn't. She wanted to keep her head in the cupboard long enough to avoid answering her mother's questions. The fact was, she would have *loved* to tell her mother why she was upset with Kyle. She would have loved to be able to talk about things with Tyler. But she couldn't, because her mother was one of the people who was part of the problem. So instead she just kept rattling the jars of spices around to make it look like she was occupied with more important matters.

"I smell turkey!"

Kate banged her head on the cupboard, but she didn't care. *Thank Goddess*, she thought. *I'm saved*. The voice belonged to her aunt Netty. Kate ran from the kitchen and into the hallway, where her aunt was taking off her coat and hanging it up. Kate ran to her and embraced her.

"You're just in time," she said.

"That bad already?" Aunt Netty answered. "What happened? Did your father eat all of the cream cheese out of the celery sticks again?"

"I wish," Kate said. "I'll tell you later," she added as the rest of her family charged into the hallway to say their hellos.

Dinner was a grim affair for Kate. Luckily, everyone was so busy chewing and talking that no one really noticed Kate's unusual silence. Kyle chattered on about his classes at school, Mrs. Morgan told Aunt Netty about the last party she'd catered and how the hostess had drunk too much champagne and started singing "Over the Rainbow," and Mr. Morgan grumbled about the after-Thanksgiving sale he was going to have at his sporting goods store and how it had been a slow year for tents. The only time Kate was even slightly interested in the conversation was when Aunt Netty told them about her latest series of tests related to her cancer and how she'd come away with a clean bill of health.

"And, of course, I'm still going to the healing circles," Netty added, winking at Kate from across the table. "They have a lot to do with this."

Kate saw her parents exchange a glance, and she saw Kyle frown, but no one commented about Aunt Netty's pronouncement. That made Kate feel a little better, but she still wanted to get Aunt Netty alone and talk to her about some things.

She got her chance after dessert. Kyle and Mr. Morgan sat on the couch to watch football and almost immediately fell asleep. Mrs. Morgan was busy putting away leftovers, and waved them away when

Kate asked if she wanted any help. "Go," her mother said. "Talk. You just mess up my system anyway."

Kate and Aunt Netty went upstairs, Kate carrying the overnight bag her aunt had brought. They went into the guest room that was always Netty's when she visited. Her aunt stretched out on the bed and sighed.

"They say there's a natural drug in turkey that makes you sleepy," she said, yawning. "Personally, I think the Pilgrims just made that up as an excuse to take naps, but I like it. Now, tell me what's up."

"I told Kyle," Kate said. "You know, about being into Wicca. He's being a jerk about it."

"I love your brother dearly," Aunt Netty said. "But open-minded is not a descriptive term that comes to mind when I think of him. Why did you tell him?"

"I thought he should know," Kate said, then saw her aunt looking at her with a knowing expression. "Okay, I wanted him to help me gang up on Mom and Dad so that they'd let me see Tyler again."

"Now it makes sense," Aunt Netty said. "And instead he made fun of you. Just like a boy."

"They're not all like that," Kate said. "Tyler's not."

"Yes, but Tyler's a *witch*, sweetie," Aunt Netty said. "Of course he's not going to be freaked out by Wicca. But imagine if you told him you wanted to pierce your nose or vote for a Republican or something else that he didn't agree with. Would he be so understanding then?"

"Okay, none of this has anything to do with why I'm mad," said Kate.

"Look," Aunt Netty said. "So Kyle is being a jerk. He'll get over it. You'll get over it. The real question is how you get your parents to agree to let you date Tyler, right?"

"Right," Kate said.

"Maybe I can help you there," Aunt Netty said. "Let me talk to your mother. I have years of experience in getting her to do things she doesn't want to."

"Thanks," Kate said.

"You don't sound very enthusiastic about it," Aunt Netty remarked.

"I'm not feeling very enthusiastic about anything lately," Kate answered. "I wish I could be more like Oggun."

"Is this some new actress I've never heard of?" Aunt Netty asked. "Like one of those Uma, Charlize, Winona things?"

"No," Kate said, smiling despite her unhappiness. "He's an orisha. A god that people who practice Santeria work with."

"You certainly are developing an interesting circle of friends," commented Aunt Netty.

"It's all part of this exercise we're doing for class," explained Kate. "We went to this ritual where some of the orishas took over the bodies of some dancers. One of them was Oggun. He kind of talked to me."

"Like I said, you know interesting people," said Aunt Netty.

"Oggun was just so sure of himself," said Kate. "I bet he'd never mope around waiting for other people to do things. He'd make them happen."

"Sounds like you need him on your side and not your frat boy brother or your loving and oh-so-attractive aunt," Netty said.

Kate looked at her. "Maybe you're right," she said. "Maybe that's exactly what I need."

Aunt Netty cocked her head. "I see the wheels turning in there," she said. "What have you got in mind?"

"I'm not sure," said Kate. "But I have an idea. What are your plans for tomorrow?"

Aunt Netty shrugged. "I'm all yours," she said.

Kate smiled. "Good," she said. "We're going to go see a woman about a god."

The next afternoon, Kate and her aunt took the bus into town and got off at the stop near Botanica Yemaya. When they walked into the store Kate saw Evelyn standing behind the counter, crumbling herbs into jars filled with water. Unidentifiable objects floated in the murky liquid.

"Hello again," Evelyn said, stepping out to kiss Kate on both cheeks. "And you have brought me a visitor."

"Evelyn, this is my aunt Netty," Kate said.

"Is she Wiccan, too?" asked Evelyn.

"No," Aunt Netty replied. "I mean, at least not officially. I go to circles from time to time."

Evelyn nodded. "Now, what can I do for you, girl?" she asked Kate. "You sounded like the devil himself was pulling at your skirts when you called me this morning."

"I wanted to talk to you about Oggun," said Kate.

"What about him?" Evelyn asked.

"Well, I've been thinking about what happened the other night," Kate told her. "When he possessed that woman and talked to me."

"Not possessed, child," Evelyn said. "He rode her. She became him. We don't go for any of that demon-inside nonsense that they talk about in the movies."

"Well, anyway," Kate said. "I've been thinking about that. Oggun is the god of war, right?"

Evelyn nodded. "That's right. And of steel and iron."

"He's brave," Kate said. "Tough. He doesn't let anyone push him around."

"He's not a bully," answered Evelyn. "But he knows what he wants."

"Well, that's what I want," Kate said. "I want to be more self-confident. I want to be able to stand up for myself and not back down."

Evelyn eyed Kate up and down. "Look at you, all full of yourself. And what do you want me to do about this?"

"I want Oggun to help me," said Kate. "I've been

reading about Santeria. I know that people think the orishas can help them if they do certain things to make them happy. I want to do that."

Evelyn looked at Aunt Netty. "This child is serious," she said.

"I think she is," agreed Aunt Netty.

Evelyn flashed Kate a big smile. "All right," she said. "We'll see what we can do. But we are going to need an omo-Oggun to help us out. Let me see what I can do."

Evelyn disappeared into the back of the store. Kate could hear the muffled voices of people talking. It went on for some time. Then Evelyn came out and waved to Kate. "Come back here," she said.

Kate and her aunt followed Evelyn into the rear of the store. Once more Kate was in the large room where the celebration had been held, although now it looked more like an ordinary storeroom. Standing there was a tall, thin man holding a broom. He looked like he was perhaps a few years older than Kate.

"This is Jon-Jon," Evelyn said, and the young man nodded a greeting. "He works for me when he's home from college. He and Papa Oggun are well acquainted."

"Evelyn says you wish to speak with Papa about a matter," said Jon-Jon in a soft voice.

"Yes," Kate said. "Is that okay?"

Jon-Jon shrugged. "Sometimes he comes, sometimes he doesn't. It is not up to me. All we can do is try."

Evelyn brought out two folding chairs and set them up. Jon-Jon sat in one and Evelyn motioned for Kate to sit in the other. Aunt Netty stood some distance behind them, watching what happened next.

Evelyn went behind Jon-Jon. She closed her eyes and began mumbling something Kate couldn't understand. She waved a black feather over Jon-Jon's head. This went on for some time, during which Jon-Jon sat perfectly still. Kate didn't notice any change in him at all, and she was sure that nothing was happening.

Then a small black dog ran into the room and sat down beside Jon-Jon's chair. It licked his hand, and suddenly Jon-Jon opened his eyes and turned them toward Kate. When he saw her he grinned widely and laughed in a voice that was nothing like Jon-Jon's soft lilt.

"Well," he said. "My child returns."

The little black dog barked excitedly, and Jon-Jon bent down and scratched it behind the ears. Seeing this, Evelyn nodded at Kate.

"Papa is very fond of dogs," she said. Then she went and stood next to Jon-Jon. "Papa Oggun, this child of yours has come with a request."

Jon-Jon looked quizzically at Kate. "And what is this request?" he asked her.

Suddenly, Kate felt very much like Dorothy in *The Wizard of Oz*. There she was, sitting in front of this amazing power that she really didn't even understand. And she wanted to ask him to help her be more brave. *I might just as well ask him for a new brain*, she thought, thinking of the Scarecrow's request of the Wizard.

"I want to be stronger," Kate said. "I want to be able to say what I think and to argue for what I think is right. I want to be more like you."

Jon-Jon roared with laughter, a rich, deep voice rolling out like waves. He slapped his knee several times, making the little dog bark with joy and put its feet on his leg. "The child wants to be like her Papa!" he cried.

He stopped laughing and placed his hands on Kate's knees. They felt much heavier than Jon-Jon's fine-boned hands should have, and once more Kate wondered just what happened when an orisha rode one of its children. Then Jon-Jon stared into her eyes for what seemed like an eternity.

"Give the child my necklace," Oggun said suddenly.

Kate saw Evelyn nod, but she had no idea what the orisha's order meant. She saw Evelyn disappear into another room and come back a moment later. She was carrying a long necklace made of small green and black beads, which she handed to Jon-Jon. He took it and placed it around Kate's neck.

"This is my necklace," he said. "Made in my colors. It marks you as my child. One day perhaps you will enter into my mysteries. For now, wear this as a reminder that you are one of my own. And as my child, you have my powers within you."

"But how do I use them?" Kate asked.

Jon-Jon smiled. "You ask the piece of Papa Oggun who lives inside of you to come out from time to time," he said. Then he leaned forward and kissed her on the cheek. When Jon-Jon leaned back in his chair, Kate saw that he looked like his old self again. The little dog sniffed his hand again, wagged its tail, then trotted off to another part of the room and lay down on the floor.

"He came, I see," said Jon-Jon, laughing gently.

"Yes," said Evelyn. "He came. He gave the child his necklace."

Jon-Jon looked at Kate approvingly. "That is very rare for one not yet initiated," he said. "You should be honored."

"I am," Kate said, fingering the beads.

"Wear that when you need Papa Oggun's presence," Evelyn told Kate.

Kate nodded. "I should pay you for this," she said.

Evelyn shook her head. "No," she replied. "But you may pay honor to Oggun. Leave him an offering of tobacco and rum tonight. That is your payment."

"Tobacco and rum," Kate repeated. "How healthy."

Evelyn and Jon-Jon both laughed. "Papa is not known for his clean living," Jon-Jon said. "But he is a good man."

Kate stood up. She thanked Jon-Jon for helping her and then walked to the front of the store with Aunt Netty and Evelyn. There they hugged good-bye.

"Thank you again," Kate said. "I really appreciate this."

"You are a friend," Evelyn said. "In Santeria we help our friends because we are all children of the orishas. Someday I may come and ask *you* for help, little sister."

Kate and Aunt Netty left the store. Kate turned to her aunt. "Where am I going to get tobacco and rum?" she asked.

Aunt Netty put her arm around Kate's shoulders. "Good thing one of us is of legal age," she said as they walked toward the corner store.

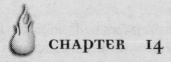

CHAPTER 14

"It was so cute," Annie said, popping a fry into her mouth. "Aunt Sarah and he were holding hands. When they saw us looking they got all embarrassed."

"My father turned *bright* red," added Becka.

"So where is all of this going?" Cooper asked, eyeing their hamburgers disdainfully as she took a bite of her garden burger.

Becka and Annie looked at one another. "We don't know," Becka said.

"But there was talk about a Christmas visit," said Annie. "I overheard that while they were doing dishes together."

"She washed, he dried," Becka said. "Isn't that the sweetest?"

"Yeah, but if this keeps up and there's a wedding, somebody is going to have to move," remarked Cooper.

"We'll worry about that if it happens," said Annie casually. But inside she replayed Cooper's comment in her mind. She was right, of course.

Somebody *would* have to move. But who would it be?

"Either way, I get a sister," Becka said. She leaned over and took one of Annie's fries. When Annie glared at her she added, "Thanks, Sis."

It was Friday night. Annie, Becka, Cooper, and Kate had all gotten together so that Becka could meet the gang. They were sitting in a booth at their favorite burger joint in town, eating and having fun. All of them except Kate, that is, who hadn't said much all night.

"What's bugging you?" Cooper asked her friend.

"It's just been a long day," replied Kate. She hadn't told them about going back to Botanica Yemaya. She didn't know why, really, except that she wanted to keep it her little secret. She was wearing her Oggun beads under her shirt, and she could feel them pressed against her skin.

"I'm sorry I didn't get to meet Sasha," said Becka.

"She and Thea went to visit Thea's family," said Cooper. "She was sort of dreading it. I guess Thea's mother is a cheek pincher."

"Ow," Becka said. "I had one of those, too. My mom's mother. I used to hate going to her house. Poor Sasha."

"You'll meet her next time," Annie told Becka. "And everyone else, too, like Sophia and Archer."

"And Tyler," Kate said.

"And Tyler," Annie repeated. She grabbed the ketchup bottle and began hammering on the end, trying to get some to come out.

"And T.J.," Cooper said quickly. "Don't forget T.J. Oh, and Jane."

"Stop," Becka said, holding up her hands. "I need a cast list to remember who's who."

"Don't worry," Annie reassured her. "We'll have everyone wear name tags."

"Kate, how was your Thanksgiving?" Cooper asked.

"Don't ask," Kate said. "Aunt Netty is here, so that's nice. But Kyle is about to get a kick in the butt."

"Her brother," Annie said to Becka.

"I came out of the broom closet to him," Kate told them. "I wanted him to help me figure out a way to convince my parents to let me start seeing Tyler again."

Annie coughed, grabbing her glass of soda and taking a big swig of it while Becka patted her on the back.

"And he didn't want to help?" asked Cooper.

Kate snorted. "No," she said shortly. "He did not want to help."

"So you haven't talked to your parents about the Tyler thing yet, then?" Annie asked.

Kate shook her head. "Not yet," she answered. "But I will."

"And what do you think they'll say?" said Becka.

"I have a good feeling about things," answered Kate, thinking about her Oggun beads and about the little bottle of rum and the cigars that were stowed in her desk drawer at home. She hoped her mother didn't look in there for anything, as she'd have a hard time explaining where the items had come from and an even harder time telling her that they'd been smuggled into the house in Aunt Netty's purse.

"I hope it all works out for you, Kate," said Annie. "I really do."

"I don't know," Kate said. "Tyler was acting kind of weird when I saw him on Tuesday. Do you know why, Annie?"

"Me?" Annie said. "No."

"I just thought you might because you're the one who talks to him the most," Kate said.

"I actually haven't talked to him in a while," replied Annie. "I've been really busy with working at Shady Hills and with school and stuff. You know how it gets."

"Well, he was kind of distant," Kate said. "I guess I can't really blame him. I mean, I haven't talked to him or hung out with him for more than half an hour at a time in months. I don't even dare e-mail him in case my parents are monitoring my on-line account. I wouldn't be surprised if he was sick of waiting."

"This conversation is getting depressing," said Becka when no one else spoke. "How about a change of subject? Cooper, how was your Turkey Day?"

"My parents are getting divorced," Cooper said flatly.

"What?" Annie exclaimed as Kate also looked shocked. "I thought they were just separating for a while so that they could work out their problems."

"So did I," Cooper said. "I guess they decided that splitting up for good was how they're going to work them out."

"Are you okay?" Annie asked.

Cooper put her hands up. "Honestly? I don't know how I am. I know it sounds weird, but I never, ever thought about my parents divorcing. They just seemed too . . . married."

"I can't imagine my parents ever getting divorced either," Kate said. "I don't know what I would do if they did."

"I know it has nothing to do with me," Cooper said. "It's all about them. But what really bothers me is if it could happen to them why couldn't it happen to me and T.J. someday." She looked at her friends' faces. "I'm not saying we're getting married," she said, making them laugh. "I'm just saying. It makes you wonder about whether or not it's all worth it."

"I think it is," Becka said. "My mother died right after I was born. I know it almost killed my father. He loved her so much. Once I asked him if he ever wished he'd never fallen in love."

"What did he say?" Kate asked.

"He said that if he hadn't he would never have gotten me," Becka said. "And he would never have the memories he does of my mother."

"Not to sound rude or anything, but that's a little

different," said Kate. "It's not like they broke up."

Becka nodded. "No," she said. "It's not. But I think it's kind of the same. Your parents aren't breaking up because they hate each other or anything, right, Cooper?"

"Right," she said. "They say that they've just grown apart."

"So they're probably feeling really sad," said Becka. "What they had didn't last, or it changed into something else. But they had it once. They experienced it. And they got you out of it."

"That's me," said Cooper. "The booby prize."

"Come on," Becka said. "I'm serious. I hate it when people break up and they say, 'I can't believe I wasted so much time with that person.' It's only wasted if you don't learn something from the experience."

"You didn't tell us she was the new Dear Abby," Cooper remarked to Annie.

"I'm from San Francisco," Becka said. "We're all touchy-feely. They don't let you live there unless you're completely self-actualized."

"I get what you're saying," Cooper told her. "I guess I just feel bad that things are changing. Maybe that's just me being selfish. But I liked my family, even when my mom was a colossal pain, which was just about every day. I still liked it. It was familiar. And now it's all going to change. No matter how much my dad says it won't, it will. I'll see him less. He'll be busy with his new life. That's just what happens."

"You're not dumping T.J., are you?" Annie asked suddenly.

"Again," added Kate.

"No, I'm not dumping T.J.," said Cooper, throwing a fry at Kate. "I've learned *something* about how to be grown up." She was tempted to tell them about her conversation with Mr. Goldstein, but for some reason she thought of that as private. Besides, she still hadn't figured out exactly what had happened that night. Talking about it would just confuse things even more. She had to let it sit for a while.

"I'm sure he'll be relieved to hear it," Kate said.

"And I'll be sure to send your regards," Cooper teased.

"So what *are* you going to do about the Tyler situation?" asked Annie, curling the paper from her straw around her finger.

"Aunt Netty is going to talk to my mother about it," Kate said. "We'll see what happens. I'm not too worried, though. Things always work out the way they're supposed to, right? I can't imagine that this isn't supposed to happen."

"Okay, so what else are we doing this evening?" Cooper asked as the waitress came to clear away their plates. "Does anybody have any big ideas?"

"Don't look at me," said Becka. "I'm the new chick. You guys are the lifers."

"We could go back to my house and play games," suggested Annie. "I know it's kind of lame, but it might be fun."

"Why not?" replied Cooper. "I'm always up for a good round of Monopoly."

"Why do I get the feeling you always want to be the little car and you buy up all the railroads?" asked Becka.

"Kate?" Annie said.

"Sure," said Kate. "Let's do that."

They paid up and left. Half an hour later they were all sitting in the same grouping they'd been in at the restaurant, only this time they were on the floor in Annie's room, eating pumpkin pie off paper plates.

"This is amazing," Cooper said, wolfing hers down.

"It's one of Ben Rowe's recipes," Annie told her.

"What's first?" asked Becka. "We have a pile of games here, girls. What's your pleasure?"

"How about we play something different?" suggested Kate suddenly.

"Like?" asked Annie.

"Truth or Dare," said Kate.

"I don't know," said Annie uncertainly. "What kind of dares would there be?"

"Nothing too weird," Kate answered. "Burping the alphabet or something. That's the fun part—making them up."

"Come on, Annie, it could be funny," Cooper said.

"And Cooper can't be the car," added Becka.

"In that case, I'm in," Annie said. "Her engine

noises are really annoying after about an hour. Who goes first?"

"I will," Cooper said. "And I pick Becka."

"I'm touched," Becka replied. "And I pick truth."

"Hmm," Cooper said. "How about this one. Have you ever stolen anything from a store?"

"Yes," Becka said instantly. "I lifted some bubble gum from the drugstore once. Okay, I didn't really steal it. I just forgot to pay them, and I went back and did it afterward. But it was sort of like stealing."

"Now it's your turn," Kate told her. "Pick someone to ask."

"Okay, I'll pick you," replied Becka. "Truth or dare?"

"Dare," said Kate assuredly.

"That's harder," Becka said. "Can Cooper and Annie help me out?"

"If they do and I do it, then they have to do it, too," Kate told her.

"Count me out," Annie said. "I'm a truth girl all the way."

"All right, then," Becka said. "I dare you to prank-call your worst enemy."

Cooper and Annie laughed. "I know who that would be," Annie said.

"Sherrie," said Cooper. "But you'll never do it."

"Won't I?" Kate told her. "Just watch."

She picked up the phone by Annie's bed and

held it in her hand thinking. "I've got it," she said, then dialed a number.

"I can't believe she's actually doing this," Annie whispered.

"I just hope they don't have caller ID," remarked Cooper.

"Hello?" Kate said, interrupting them. "Is this Sherrie Adams?" She was attempting to disguise her voice, and not doing a very good job of it because she kept trying not to laugh. "This is the emergency butt repair service. Yes, that's right. We're coming right over. We hear you have a big crack in yours."

Kate hung up and fell on the floor laughing. The others shrieked as well, and soon they were all in hysterics.

"That was *so* dumb," Cooper said, wiping tears of laughter from her cheeks. "That was a total five-year-old-boy joke."

"But so funny," quipped Becka.

"Okay," Kate said, regaining her composure. "Now it's my turn. I pick Annie."

Annie raised her hand. "You already know my choice," she said. "Truth, truth, truth."

"Let me see," Kate said thoughtfully. "What would I like to know about Miss Annie Crandall?"

She looked at Annie with interest, as if she were examining a statue or something. Then she snapped her fingers. "Got it," she said. "If you could date any guy we all know, who would it be?"

Cooper and Becka looked at Annie, who had

turned a vibrant shade of red and was stammering. "I—I—I— don't know," she said. "Does it have to be someone we *know* know, or can it be someone we know *of*? Because I mean Ben Affleck is really cute or maybe Johnny Depp except not in that movie where he cries all the time. Oh, or what about that one from 'N SYNC. You know, the one with the cat eyes. How about him?"

"No," Kate said. "It has to be someone we all know personally. Like some guy at school. Or even a teacher. Just someone we know. Who would you most like to go out with?"

Annie looked at the three of them, her brow furrowed. "I don't know," she said. "It's not like I *like* that many people."

"Come on," Kate said. "There must be one or two you think about sometimes."

"Okay," Annie said. "Yeah, I'm sure there is. I just have to think about it. Oh, I know. How about Mr. Malcolmson?"

"The physics teacher?" Cooper said, wrinkling her nose. "Isn't he, like, seventy-two or something?"

"Well, you all rushed me," Annie said, sounding flustered. "It was the first name that popped into my head."

"You're sure that's your answer?" asked Kate.

"No," Annie said. "I mean yes. Is it my turn now?"

Kate nodded. Annie turned to Cooper. "What's your favorite band?" she asked.

"That's not a good question!" objected Cooper. "You're supposed to ask something that could be embarrassing, or at least funny."

"I'm sorry," Annie said. "I'm just not very good at this game."

"Fine," Cooper said. "In that case, this week my favorite band would be Apples in Stereo."

"This isn't going as well as I thought it would," said Kate. "I vote we switch to Monopoly."

"I get to be the car!" Cooper shouted.

Annie eagerly opened the game box and began taking out the pieces. "Finally," she said. "A game I'm good at."

Kate reached over and took the little metal top hat. "You mean *another* one," she said.

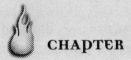

CHAPTER 15

"Annie and Tyler are fooling around behind my back."

Dr. Hagen looked at Kate, her eyes registering surprise. Privately, Kate smiled to herself. It was hard to get her therapist to show emotion. She was, after all, supposed to be a neutral observer. But Kate could tell that the usually staid doctor had been shocked by her sudden pronouncement.

"Are you sure?" the therapist asked.

"I don't have hard proof or anything," Kate replied. "But I'm pretty sure."

"What are you basing this on?" Dr. Hagen said.

"Women's intuition," answered Kate. "They've both been acting really strangely lately. Whenever I bring up Tyler's name Annie gets all flustered. I've had enough crushes to know when someone has one on someone else."

"What about Tyler?" the doctor continued. "Why do you think he returns this crush—if, in fact, Annie really has one on him?"

Kate sighed. "Boys act nervous when there's something they don't want you to know. I just put two and two together. I mean, after all, Tyler and Annie have been spending a lot of time together ever since my parents said that I couldn't see him. I guess I'm not surprised, really."

"But you're feeling something," said Dr. Hagen. "Otherwise you wouldn't have brought it up."

"I'm not sure what I'm feeling," replied Kate. "I've been thinking about it a lot. And you're right— I don't know for sure. That makes it even harder, because I don't know whether or not I should be angry at them or sad that Tyler apparently doesn't want to be with me anymore."

"So what do you think you should do about it?"

"I just really don't know," Kate answered. "I'm going to think about it."

"That seems like a mature decision," Dr. Hagen remarked.

"Isn't it?" said Kate. "I think I've learned a lot from our little chats."

The therapist looked at Kate over the top of her little round glasses. "I'll have to dock you fifteen penalty points for that comment," she said.

Kate laughed. "I thought you might like that."

"I must say, your attitude seems to have changed since we last saw one another," said Dr. Hagen. "You're much more—"

"Confident?" Kate suggested.

"Yes," the doctor said, nodding her head. "Much

more confident. Why the change?"

"Let's just say I had a talk with a friend," she answered.

The doctor looked at her curiously but didn't ask anything more about the subject. Kate thought about the necklace of green and black beads beneath her shirt and leaned back in her chair, content.

"Do you want to talk some more about your suspicions of a romantic relationship between Tyler and Annie?" Dr. Hagen asked.

"If you do," Kate said.

The doctor tapped her pencil on her notebook. "You and Annie are very close," she said. "And bonds between friends, especially girlfriends, can often be much more intense even than the bonds between romantic partners. You and Annie have also been through a lot together in terms of your involvement in Wicca. If what you suspect is true, how do you think that will affect your relationship with her?"

"I won't be able to trust her," Kate said quickly. "How could I?"

"Do you think you could remain friends with her?"

"I really don't know," Kate said. "It would be really, really hard. When you work with people doing magic, you have to be able to trust them. If I couldn't trust her, what would be the point?"

"So your involvement in Wicca would be changed as well?" asked Dr. Hagen.

"I wouldn't stop studying it because of this," Kate said. "But I would probably have to stop practicing it with Annie. Or with Tyler, for that matter. How could I ever be in a coven with him, knowing what he did?"

"These are all enormous questions," the therapist told her. "They'll probably take some time to work through and figure out."

"Oh, good," Kate said brightly. "That means you and I will be spending even *more* time together."

Dr. Hagen put down her pad and pencil and folded her hands. "I'm pleased that you're so looking forward to it," she said. "Has anyone ever told you that sarcasm is often a cover for deep-seated anger?"

"No," Kate replied. "Never."

Later that day, while her brother was out with some friends, her aunt was taking a nap, and her parents were busy with their own pursuits, Kate went downtown to Crones' Circle. After peering in the window to make sure that Tyler—or anyone else she didn't particularly want to see—wasn't there, she went inside. She was happy to see that Archer was working the counter. When Archer saw her come in she smiled broadly. "Hey there. What brings you in, and where are your cohorts?"

"I'm solo today," Kate replied. "I came in looking for something to go with my assignment for class."

"A book?" asked Archer.

Kate shook her head. "Music," she said. "I'm

studying Santeria, and last weekend I went to this ritual over at Botanica Yemaya. They played drums, and I really liked them. I was wondering if there were any recordings of that kind of stuff."

Archer came out from behind the counter. "Let's check the CDs," she said. "I know we have a lot of drum music, but I don't know if any of it is specifically Santerian."

Kate followed Archer to the CD racks, and they began looking. Archer was right—there *were* a lot of drumming CDs. But most of them were either Native American or a blend of New Age cultures. Then, just as she was about give up, Kate saw something. She picked up the CD and looked at it. *"Hearts of the Saints,"* she read. The cover showed several large African-type drums with what looked like spirits coming out of them.

Kate turned the CD over. "This magical recording captures the essence of a traditional Santerian *tambor*, or gathering," she read out loud.

Kate looked at Archer. "This is *exactly* what I was looking for," she said. "Thanks."

"So you're having a good time with this assignment, then?" Archer asked as they walked back to the counter so that Kate could pay.

"I am," Kate said. "It's really interesting. A lot of it is like Wicca, but a lot of it isn't. It's cool seeing how other people do things."

"When I did my year and a day and had to do this assignment I picked Sufi mysticism," Archer said. "At first I wasn't sure about it, but the more I read and the more I met people who were into it, the more I fell in love with it. I still am."

"But you stayed with Wicca," Kate said.

"Yes," said Archer. "When it comes down to it, I'm at home in the Craft. I appreciate bits and pieces of many different paths, but they aren't my paths. Witchcraft is. One of my big breakthroughs during that year was realizing that it was okay to take pieces from other traditions and use them if they work for you. You just have to do it with respect for the tradition, otherwise it's just kind of stealing."

"I never thought of it like that," said Kate, taking her change and her bag from Archer.

"Have fun with the CD," Archer told her. "We'll see you on Tuesday, right?"

"Oh, I wouldn't miss it for anything," replied Kate. "Bye."

She left the store and walked back to the bus stop. As she walked she thought about what Archer had just said about borrowing from different traditions. She was definitely borrowing from Santeria. But it wasn't like she'd done it on purpose. After all, Oggun had chosen *her* as his child, right? She hadn't chosen him. So why shouldn't she take advantage of that?

There's no reason you shouldn't, she told herself as she stood waiting for her bus home.

When she arrived at her house a little while later, everyone was putting on their coats.

"There you are," her mother said. "We're all

going to go to a movie. Do you want to come?"

Kate thought for a moment. "What are you going to see?"

"The new Meg Ryan," Aunt Netty said.

"Oh," Kate said, feigning disappointment. "I saw that with Annie and Cooper last week. But you guys go. It's really good. And I'm kind of wiped out anyway. I'm going to take a nap."

"Are you sure?" asked her mother. "We can always see a different movie."

"No," Kate said. "You go. We'll do something tonight when you get back."

"We'll bring home pizza," Mr. Morgan said. "How does that sound?"

"Perfect," said Kate.

"Okay, honey," her mother said. "We'll see you later."

Kate waited for them all to leave. Then, when she saw the car pulling out of the driveway and she was sure they were gone, she went upstairs to her room and shut the door. Kyle hadn't gone with them, and she wasn't sure when he might get back from spending the day with his buddies. She didn't want to have what she was planning to do get interrupted.

She took the CD out of the bag and ripped the cellophane wrapping from it. Putting it in her CD player, she punched in track eight and hit Play. The room was filled with the sound of drums. They started out slow and steady, the beat regular and heavy. It sounded like something—or someone—

was walking very heavily. Each slap of the drum was like a foot hitting the floor. Almost instantly Kate pictured Oggun as a large, heavy man stamping his feet. The image made her smile, and she laughed.

As the music played she readied the room. First she got out some candles, which she placed on her dresser, her desk, and anywhere there was a flat surface free of papers and anything else that might catch fire. She lit them and then turned off the electric lights so that the room was filled only with candlelight.

Then she went to her closet and pulled out a dress. It was sort of like the ones she'd seen many of the women wearing at the ritual at Botanica Yemaya, although it was red instead of white. She'd bought it for a garden party the year before and hadn't worn it since. Now she stripped off her clothes and pulled the dress over her head. She turned around, feeling it move around her body. *This is perfect*, she told herself.

She walked to her desk and took out the bundle that she'd hidden there. Opening it, she removed one of the cigars and the little bottle of rum. She opened the rum and poured it into a small glass she'd taken from the kitchen. This she set in front of one of the candles on her desk, placing the cigar alongside it. She didn't have any image of Oggun, but since he was the orisha of steel she had bought a small knife at the hardware store. This she placed with the other objects on the makeshift altar.

Then she went and stood in the middle of her room, surrounded by the candles and listening to the drums. The song had gotten faster, and the beats more complicated. There were at least three different drums playing at once, each pounding out a different rhythm. It was like they were talking to one another, calling out and responding with their voices like children playing in a field.

Kate closed her eyes and swayed gently. The dress swished around her legs as she moved in time to the music. She didn't really know what she was doing. She just knew that she wanted to feel the music of Oggun. She wanted to feel what the people at the ritual had felt. She wanted to feel power.

She emptied her mind and let the music fill it, allowing the rhythms to take over. Then, slowly, she moved her body in time with what she heard. She lifted her foot and put it down again as one of the drums let out a sharp snap. Then she raised the other foot and did the same thing again, although this time she bent forward at the waist, letting her head hang down.

At first she felt ridiculous. *You have no idea what to do*, she chided herself. But she'd done enough rituals, and been in enough unfamiliar situations, that she knew the best approach was to just let go and see what happened. So that's what she did. She allowed her hands, feet, and head to move with the drums. She lifted her arms and twisted. She grabbed her dress and moved it around her legs. She became the person the music was calling to.

She'd put the CD track on repeat, and soon it began again. This time Kate knew what she was going to hear and remembered some of it. She was able to dance more smoothly and freely, and soon she was stamping her feet, waving her hands, and moving around the room with the drums pulling her and pushing her, first one way and then another. But she didn't feel like she was being controlled by them. She felt like she was part of their song, and that felt wonderful.

At the point where the drums were the loudest and most furious, Kate put out her hands and began to spin. She twirled around and around, never stumbling. She felt like a toy that someone was spinning faster and faster. She was somehow connected to the sky by an invisible string that held her up and prevented her from falling. She felt light and free and happy.

The green and black beaded necklace slipped out of the front of her dress as she spun. It twirled with her, and she held on to it, feeling the small beads beneath her fingers. She was dancing for Oggun, and she knew that he was happy about it. She could feel his presence in the room, called by the drums and by her dancing.

Gradually she stopped spinning and went to her desk, where the offerings of rum and tobacco sat by the steel blade of the knife. "Papa Oggun," Kate said. "Please help me." She hadn't planned this part of the ritual. She'd only intended to dance. But now she was overcome by the energy she'd raised, and she had an idea.

"Oggun," she said. "I need your help." She paused, uncertain of how to proceed. Vague thoughts had formed in her head as she'd danced, and now they were becoming clearer. She knew what she wanted. She just wasn't sure how to ask for it.

"I want the truth about Tyler and Annie to come out," she said. "I want to know what they're doing. Help me find out." She paused a moment, uncertain of whether or not to continue. There was something else that had been on her mind, something else she wanted to ask. But she wasn't sure it was something she should do.

She started to turn away from the little altar on her desk without saying anything else. She'd asked for enough. But then she stopped and turned back. Maybe she *should* do it, she thought. After all, fair was fair, and magic was all about balance.

She looked at the cigar and the rum. She pictured Papa Oggun smoking the cigar, blowing smoke rings out of his mouth before taking a drink. She pictured him smiling at her. "Ask me, child," she heard him say in her mind.

She took a breath. The drums pounded in her head. "If they *are* cheating on me," she said. "Then I want them to be punished for it."

CHAPTER 16

"I think it's important that we all talk about this."

Cooper looked at her father. She was sitting on the couch, pressed as tightly as she could get against the arm farthest away from her mother, who was at the other end holding a glass of water and looking very worn out. Mr. Rivers was sitting in one of the armchairs across from them, nervously tapping his hands on his knees as he looked at his wife and daughter.

"I know this is stressful on all of us," said Mr. Rivers. "It's not an easy time, and it's not going to get easier for a while. But if we can *talk* about what's happening, then I think we'll be doing ourselves a lot of good."

Neither Cooper nor her mother said anything in response. Cooper's throat was dry, and what she wanted most was a drink of water like her mother had. But she didn't want to get up to get it, and she didn't want to ask her mother for a sip of hers. So she sat there, a dry tickle in the back of her throat, and wished she was dead instead.

"I'm going to come this weekend and take some things out of the house," Mr. Rivers continued. "Your mother and I think it would be better if she isn't here when that happens, so she's going to spend the day elsewhere. Cooper, you're free to stay or go—whatever you think is best."

Cooper shrugged. "Why would I go?" she asked. "It's your stuff."

Her father nodded. "We just thought maybe you would be uncomfortable," he said.

Cooper sighed. "I'm not six," she said. "I'm sixteen. I know what a divorce is. I know you guys don't hate each other. I know this has nothing to do with me. I've seen the after-school specials. I've read Judy Blume. I *get* it."

"You seem very angry about it for someone who gets it," remarked her mother.

"I'm angry because it really sucks that this is happening," Cooper said. "I'm not going to pretend that I'm not. But I'm not mad at you guys or at myself or anything like that. I think you're the ones who are having the problem with it."

Her father and mother exchanged glances but didn't say anything. Cooper rearranged herself, drawing her leg up under her and holding one of the couch pillows to her chest.

"Look," she said. "I appreciate you trying to make this easy on me. I really do. But it's not helping. Dad, I know you have to take your stuff out of here. Mom,

I know it's going to be hard living with just the two of us in the house. But that's what's going to happen, and I'll deal with it. We'll all deal with it."

She stopped talking. She hoped she hadn't made her parents angry by lecturing them in that way, but she couldn't stand sitting there listening to her father sound like he was leading some kind of encounter group for even another second.

"Well," her father said. "I guess that's really what it all comes down to, isn't it? We'll deal with it."

Cooper had never heard her father sound so sad. She wondered just how tough the separation and impending divorce were on her parents. Even though they clearly wanted to end their marriage, she imagined that they must be stressed out by everything that would have to be done.

"We just want you to know that we're here for you if you need us," Mr. Rivers said quietly. "Both of us."

Cooper glanced at her mother when she heard her father say that. She knew what he was getting at. Mrs. Rivers was more like her daughter than either of them liked to admit. They both found it difficult to talk about their feelings. This was made even more difficult by the fact that they disagreed on so many topics, including Cooper's involvement in Wicca. Living alone with her mother was *not* going to be easy. Cooper knew that.

"Yes," Mrs. Rivers said after a moment. "That's right."

"Thanks," said Cooper. "Can I go now? I have someplace else I'd rather be."

Mr. Rivers nodded. Cooper put down the pillow and got up. She walked to her father, leaned down, and kissed him. "I love you, Daddy," she said.

Mr. Rivers looked up at her, surprised. Cooper knew that it was because she hadn't called him Daddy since she was a little girl. "I love you, too, sweetie," he said, his voice choking.

Cooper turned to her mother. "And I love you, too," she said, bending and giving her a hug. "Remember that the next time we have some big fight."

"I will," her mother said. "And you do the same."

"Okay then," Cooper said. "I think my work is done here. I'll be back later."

She left her parents sitting in the living room and went upstairs to her bedroom. There she grabbed her guitar case, backpack, and keys, and left again. She went downstairs and out the front door, not looking to see if her parents were still sitting in stony silence in the other room. She knew that they would have to work out whatever their issues were without her.

She got into her Nash Metropolitan convertible and drove to T.J.'s house. When she went to the door and rang the bell, the McAllisters big Irish setter, Mac, started to bark happily. A moment later Mrs. McAllister opened the door.

"What are you doing still ringing the bell?" she

asked when she saw Cooper standing there. "Just come in next time."

"Hey, Mrs. M.," Cooper said, going inside.

"And for the love of Mary, call me Mom," Mrs. McAllister said as she shut the door. "You're practically one of mine anyway now that you've got two of my boys smitten with you."

"Two?" Cooper asked as she set her guitar case down and took off her jacket.

"T.J. and Dylan," Mrs. McAllister replied. "He hasn't stopped talking about you since he was here."

Cooper smiled. It was Dylan who had talked sense into both T.J. and Cooper when they had been thinking of splitting up. "How is he?" asked Cooper.

"Fine," T.J.'s mother said. "He and his special friend are about to celebrate their anniversary, so he's all excited about the party."

Cooper laughed. She knew that no matter how many times they asked her to, Mrs. McAllister still couldn't call Dylan's partner his boyfriend. Once, when T.J. had teased her about it, her pale Irish skin had flared up almost to the color of her fiery hair and she'd said fiercely, "I'm not going to call the grown man my son is living with his boyfriend. For the love of Mike, the two of them have been together longer than most married couples I know. He stopped being a boyfriend a long time ago. So until they come up with a better word, he's Dylan's special friend and that's that."

"T.J.!" Mrs. McAllister called. "Get your lazy self down here and greet your girlfriend properly." Then she turned to Cooper. "I know what you're thinking, but you *are* his girlfriend, special or not."

Cooper laughed, and Mrs. McAllister returned to the kitchen, where from the smell of things she was making her famous corned beef and cabbage. Cooper, a staunch vegetarian, had been afraid of refusing to eat T.J.'s mother's signature dish when invited to her first Sunday dinner there. But Mrs. McAllister had made her a separate batch prepared with tofu instead and served it without a word. That had been the moment when Cooper knew she'd been accepted into the tight-knit McAllister clan.

"Hey there," T.J. said, coming into the room.

"Ready to make some music?" asked Cooper.

"Sure thing," replied T.J.

The two of them walked through the kitchen, where Mrs. McAllister was standing over the stove and watching the various pots she had going like some kind of mad scientist working up an experiment. "Don't be too long in there," she told them. "Dinner will be ready in an hour or so."

"We'll be back," T.J. said.

"And not too much kissing," his mother added as they were opening the door to the garage.

T.J. and Cooper turned and looked at her. "I was sixteen once, too, you know," Mrs. McAllister said. "And *my* family had a garage, too. Just ask your father."

T.J. and Cooper laughed and went through the door.

"Can you believe her?" T.J. asked as they plugged in their guitars and tuned up.

"She's an original," agreed Cooper. "I wish my mother had half of her spark."

"How are things with your parents anyway?" T.J. said.

"About what you would expect," answered Cooper. "Sometimes I wish they would throw things or at least yell. But they'll be fine."

T.J. nodded. "What do you want to work on?" he asked.

Cooper loved that T.J. had asked about her parents and then dropped the subject when she indicated that she didn't really have anything to say about it. He always knew when to leave her alone and when to push her a little bit.

"Let's play Follow the Leader tonight," Cooper said. "I don't feel like thinking too much."

"Sounds good to me," T.J. replied. "You go first."

Follow the Leader was a game she and T.J. had invented when they first started playing together. Whoever went first played the opening notes of a famous song. The other person had to recognize it and see if she or he could play the whole song as well. Then it was that person's turn to pick a song, but to make the game even harder, whoever was choosing the next song had to go right into it from the old one. There was no stopping or starting.

Cooper loved the game. Not only did it force her to learn a lot of cool music, but it taught her to think on her feet. She and T.J. both loved to try to stump each other with difficult or obscure songs. But they both listened to a lot of music, so they knew all kinds of stuff.

Cooper thought for a minute, trying to pick something good to start with. Then she began playing some chords. When he heard them, T.J. laughed. "'Wild Thing,'" he said. "How easy."

He joined in with Cooper, his bass line chugging along beneath her guitar work. They played for a couple of minutes and then suddenly T.J. started playing something new. Cooper listened to it and knew it instantly—the Rolling Stones' "Brown Sugar."

"You'll have to do better than that," she teased as she played the song along with him. The Stones were one of her favorite bands, even if they were older than her parents were. She had learned a lot about playing guitar from listening to their records, and this song was one she really enjoyed.

For her next choice Cooper tried to fool T.J. by playing something relatively new. And for a moment she thought she had him when he looked at her blankly. But just as their one-minute time limit for the other person to start playing was about to run out, he called out, "Matchbox Twenty!" and joined in. Cooper bared her teeth at him in pretend anger and kept playing.

They went back and forth for the better part of an hour, each of them trying to trip the other one up. They played songs by old groups and new ones, rock bands and country bands, hits and songs that only people who *really* listened to everything on an album would know.

Finally, T.J. started playing something that Cooper didn't immediately recognize. He stood there, playing and grinning like a fool, taunting her by glancing at his watch every few seconds. Cooper racked her brain, trying to figure out where she might have heard the song. But nothing about it was jogging any memories. Finally, T.J. made a sound like a buzzer going off.

"Time's up!" he crowed. "You lose."

"Aaahhhh!" Cooper said. "What was it?"

"ABBA!" T.J. replied. "'Does Your Mother Know?'"

"ABBA?" repeated Cooper. "Since when have *you* ever owned an ABBA CD?"

"I don't," T.J. admitted. "But Mike does, and he was playing it all weekend while he was home from college. I decided to learn something just for this kind of occasion."

"Unfair!" Cooper said. "You used a bad Swedish pop song on purpose. Evil, evil man."

"All's fair in Follow the Leader," T.J. said.

"You just wait," Cooper told him. "I'm going to brush up on my Cher songs and kick your butt next time."

T.J. replied by starting to play the opening notes of the old Sonny and Cher song "I've Got You, Babe." Cooper rolled her eyes and unslung her guitar. "You're a freak," she said.

T.J. put down his guitar as well, and the two of them went back inside. Mrs. McAllister was just dishing up dinner when they arrived.

"That was some racket the two of you were making in there," she said. "Why can't you learn some nice songs?"

"Because nice songs aren't fun to play," T.J. told her, reaching for a piece of corned beef that was on the platter by the stove.

Mrs. McAllister slapped his hand with her wooden spoon. "You wash those," she said. "Then go sit down."

T.J. and Cooper laughed and went to do as she'd told them. Minutes later they were seated at the McAllisters' big dining room table. Cooper and T.J. sat on one side, with T.J.'s brother Mike on the other and Mr. and Mrs. McAllister at either end. As the dishes were passed around the table, Mac ran from seat to seat, sticking his big nose into laps and onto the table and sniffing.

"That dog is worse than any of you boys ever were," Mrs. McAllister said, shooing Mac away.

"But he doesn't *talk*," remarked Mr. McAllister.

"And *that* is a blessing."

"How long are you home for, Mike?" asked Cooper as she spooned food onto her plate.

"I have to drive back to school after dinner," T.J.'s brother answered. He was practically shoveling food into his mouth as he spoke, and his mother looked at him disapprovingly.

"Is that how they teach you to eat at that place?" she asked. "You're giving McAllisters everywhere a bad name."

"There are ten billion of us," Mike shot back. "One of us is bound to give the others a bad name, so it might as well be me."

"Do you hear your son?" Mrs. McAllister asked her husband.

Mr. McAllister shrugged and put a piece of carrot in his mouth. "You're half responsible for him," he said. "How do you know your half isn't the bad half?"

Everyone laughed at his joke, especially Cooper. It had taken her a while to get used to the way the McAllisters spoke to one another, mainly because it was so different from the formal way her family usually interacted. But once she had realized that they were able to joke like that because they all really loved and respected one another, she had thoroughly enjoyed it. It made her feel like she was with a real family, one where she was welcome and nobody expected anything from her.

"You don't see Cooper eating like a wild hog,

now, do you?" Mrs. McAllister said.

"That's because she's eating that tofu stuff," Mike protested. "Who would *want* to eat that?"

"It gives her horrible gas," remarked T.J.

Cooper smacked him on the arm. "You are so full of it!" she said. "And at least I don't down a whole can of Coke and then pretend I'm making moose calls."

They continued the good-natured bickering all through dinner, in between laughing at one another's jokes and complimenting Mrs. McAllister on her cooking. When it was all over, Cooper and T.J. helped clear the table. Then Cooper volunteered to help Mrs. McAllister wash up. "You go talk to Mike before he leaves," she told T.J.

When they were alone and Cooper was drying the dishes as Mrs. McAllister handed them to her, Cooper suddenly found it hard to talk as easily as she had at dinner. Finally, Mrs. McAllister said, "T.J. told me about your parents. I'm sorry to hear about it."

"Thanks," Cooper said, realizing suddenly that she'd wanted to help T.J's mother for that very reason. It made her feel normal again. They continued washing and drying in silence for a minute. Then Cooper asked, "This isn't any of my business, but have you and Mr. McAllister ever thought about splitting up?"

Mrs. McAllister laughed. "Of course we have," she said. "But we're Irish, dear. We never divorce. Then we wouldn't have anything to complain about."

Cooper snorted as Mrs. McAllister laughed at her own joke. Then T.J.'s mother turned serious and sighed. "We've had our rough patches," she said. "But every marriage does. Every *relationship* does, whether you're friends or siblings or what have you. There are days when I'm sure all of my boys wish they were orphans, and there are days when I wish I was one of those skinny supermodels with lots of rich men after me instead of that husband of mine asking where his clean underpants are for the third time in an hour. But I love them all, and I wouldn't trade them for anything."

"I guess that's the difference between you and my parents," Cooper remarked.

"Don't be so hard on them," Mrs. McAllister said. "People can love each other without being in love with each other. Even married people. It takes brave people to recognize that."

"I know," Cooper said. "I'm really *not* mad at them. I just get scared sometimes that I'll be like them."

"Only if you let yourself," Mrs. McAllister said, handing her the last dish to dry.

When they were done, Cooper surprised herself by giving T.J.'s mother a hug and a kiss on the cheek, just as she had her own parents. But this time it was for a different reason. "Thank you for making me feel at home," she said.

"Please, girl," Mrs. McAllister said. "I need someone to help me stand up to these awful men."

Cooper left the kitchen and found Mike getting ready to leave. He was carrying his bags to his car, and T.J. was helping him.

"I should get home, too," Cooper said. "I've got some stuff to do before school starts up again tomorrow."

T.J. nodded. "You mean you have to look through your CDs and find something I'll never recognize," he said, grinning.

Cooper smiled. "Come here," she said, opening her arms.

"Is this a trick?" asked T.J. suspiciously.

"Just come here," said Cooper again.

T.J. went to her, and she put her arms around him. "There's something I want to tell you," she said.

"A good something or a bad something?" T.J. asked.

"A good something," Cooper replied. "I love you."

T.J. pulled away slightly and looked at her. "Did you just say what I think you said?" he asked.

Cooper nodded. "Don't sound so shocked."

T.J. laughed. "I just never expected you to be the one to say it first," he said.

"That's not what you're supposed to say back," said Cooper.

T.J. hugged her tightly. "I love you, too," he said. "And I'm glad you said it first."

"Okay," Cooper said. "Let's not make a big thing out of this."

They stood there holding each other for a few minutes, neither of them saying anything. But although her mouth was silent, Cooper's mind was racing with emotions. She wanted to cry. She wanted to laugh. She wanted to sing and shout and run until she fell into an exhausted heap of happiness. She was so excited that she felt like she might burst if T.J. let go of her, the thrill of being in love and being loved back was so strong in her.

You did it, she told herself. *You listened to Mr. Goldstein. You looked for the love and grabbed it.* And as she felt T.J.'s heart beating alongside her own, she knew that, as Mr. Goldstein had promised her, love would help her get through anything.

CHAPTER 17

I know she knows something, Annie kept telling herself. *First she said that thing at my house the other night, and then in school today she was all weird, too. It's like she's just waiting for me to break.*

It was Monday afternoon. Annie was at Shady Hills. She was working in the kitchen, helping chop vegetables for dinner. Since she was so good at cooking, she had listed kitchen help as one of the things she would like to do. Until that afternoon they'd never assigned her to it, but now she was happy to just stand in one spot cutting up carrots and celery. It was mindless work, and it gave her time to think.

What she was thinking about was Kate. Ever since Kate had made the comment about Annie's being good at games, Annie had been paranoid. Kate hadn't said anything else about it. But she'd asked the question about who Annie would most like to go out with. *Why would she ask that if she didn't suspect something was going on?* Annie asked herself.

And Kate had been friendly but distant at school, making Annie even more nervous.

Annie had even called Tyler to ask him if he'd said anything to Kate. He'd sworn that he hadn't. And the only other people who knew anything about the situation were Cooper and Becka, and Annie knew that neither of them had said anything to Kate.

That was another thing—she was missing Becka. When Becka and her father had left the night before, Annie had felt sad. She'd really enjoyed having Becka there for the holiday, and she'd enjoyed having Mr. Dunning there as well, although she hadn't seen very much of him. He and Aunt Sarah had spent most of their time together. But even though it was a brief visit, the two of them already felt like family to Annie. She'd grilled her aunt about what was going on with her and Mr. Dunning, but Aunt Sarah had simply smiled and said, "Isn't he a nice man?"

Everyone is playing games with me, thought Annie. She really did feel like her world was spinning around and around and she was waiting for it to stop so she could get her bearings. The thing with Tyler had been bad enough when she was the only one worrying about it. But now it was worse because she'd told several people and she couldn't help but wonder whether or not *they* had already talked or might tell someone they shouldn't. She hated feeling like that, and she wished she could just shake her head and clear it.

She chopped at the pile of carrots on her cutting board, neatly dicing them into little cubes. She pushed the pile along with the ends of her fingers cupped against the wooden board, just as she'd taught herself to do from watching cooking shows on TV. As the carrots were pushed toward the sharp steel blade of the knife, on the other side they came out as perfectly square bits ready to be put into the dish the cook was making.

If only I was as good at managing my life as I am at cooking, things would be much easier, she thought as she started on another bunch of carrots. *What am I going to do?* Becka had said not to tell Kate anything, and Annie really wanted to believe that that was the best approach to the situation. But Kate was obviously aware that *something* was up, even if she didn't know the details. How long would it be before she figured it out? *Maybe it would be better to just tell her now,* thought Annie. But just thinking about that made her stomach hurt. How could she ever look Kate in the face and tell her that she'd kissed Tyler?

All of a sudden she felt a sharp pain in her hand. She looked down and saw something red splashed against the orange of the carrots. The effect was startling, and she was so fascinated by the brightness of the red that it was another few moments before she felt a searing pain and realized that she'd cut herself. She held up her hand and saw a deep cut going through her index finger. Blood ran from it and dripped onto the half-finished pile of carrots on the cutting board.

Annie grabbed a dishrag from the counter nearby and held it to her hand. She knew that she had to stop the bleeding, and she remembered reading somewhere that putting pressure on it was the best way to do that. So she held the towel tightly around her finger, trying to ignore the throbbing pain that radiated through her hand and into her arm.

It will be okay, she told herself. *It's just a cut. You've had cuts before.*

She looked at the towel and saw that it was dark with blood that was soaking through from the cut. She knew that a regular cut wouldn't bleed that much. Something was wrong. Gently she unwound the towel to look at the damage to her finger and found that the wound was still bleeding freely. The skin gaped open slightly, and she could see that the cut went almost to the bone.

"Marge!" Annie called to the kitchen director. "I've got to go see the nurse."

Marge heard her and came running over. When she saw the blood-soaked towel she put her hand to her mouth. "Go, honey," she said. "Get down there right now. Do you want someone to help you?"

Annie shook her head. "I'm okay," she said. "I think I just need a Band-Aid."

She left the kitchen and walked down the hall. Luckily, the nurses' office wasn't too far, and she was there in under a minute. But when the nurse on duty looked up from her desk and saw Annie standing there with blood dripping from her bandaged hand, she stood up immediately.

"Sit down," she ordered, leading Annie to an examination table at the back of the room.

Annie climbed onto the table and sat, her legs hanging over the end. She watched as the nurse peeled the grisly towel away and looked at the finger beneath it.

"How'd you manage this?" she asked.

"I was cutting vegetables in the kitchen," answered Annie. "The knife must have slipped."

"This is going to require stitches," the nurse said.

"Stitches?" said Annie. "But it's just a cut."

"A cut that goes almost to the bone," replied the nurse. "Now, you just sit there and don't move. I'm going to have to get one of the residents to do this."

The nurse left, leaving Annie to contemplate her cut finger. How had it happened? She was usually so careful when it came to working in the kitchen. The most she'd ever had was a small cut from trying to peel a lemon with a knife. But this was bad. Even she could see that now. In fact, she was feeling kind of queasy looking at it. It was as if the knife had had a mind of its own, like it had *wanted* to cut her.

The nurse came back in, accompanied by a young man. "There she is," the nurse said.

The man came over and inspected Annie's finger. "Hi," he said. "I'm Dr. Albion."

"Hi," said Annie stupidly. There were always residents at the home. They came there to learn about geriatric medicine, then left when their stays were over, to be replaced by new residents. Annie seldom knew their names, mainly because she liked to stay as far away from the infirmary as possible.

"This is a bad cut," said Dr. Albion. "But I'll stitch it up and you'll be fine. Just let me get the things I'll need."

He went to the cupboard at the back of the room and returned a minute later with a small plastic container holding various things. As he laid them out on the white paper cloth that covered the tray he was working on, Annie felt herself getting nervous. There were small curved needles, lengths of black thread, and gauze pads. Worst of all, there was a hypodermic needle.

"What's that for?" asked Annie when the doctor picked up the needle.

"It's to numb the area," he explained. "It's best if you don't watch. I'm going to have to give you a couple of pokes."

Annie shut her eyes, waiting for the first needle stick. When it came, she let out a little yelp. It hurt more than she'd expected, and the sharp sting of the needle was followed by an even more unpleasant burning sensation. She bit her lip and hoped it would go away soon.

Dr. Albion gave her two more shots. Luckily, they seemed to be working, and soon her finger did indeed feel numb. The doctor poked her skin lightly with the end of the needle. "Can you feel that?" he asked.

"No," Annie said.

"Good," the doctor replied. "Now we can get down to business."

Annie watched as he picked up one of the small curved needles with a length of black thread pulled through it. She didn't want to look, but she couldn't pull her eyes away as he pushed the end of the needle through her skin and then brought it back up on the other side of the cut. When he pulled the thread through after it, she watched as her skin was pulled together.

"You'll probably have a scar here," the doctor said as he worked. "This is a deep cut, and fingers don't always heal really well because we bend them so much. But just be glad you didn't sever any nerves or anything."

Annie tried to be glad, but she couldn't be. Even with the anesthetic she'd been given, having her finger sewn up hurt. She couldn't tell if the pain was real or imagined, but every time Dr. Albion pulled the thread through she felt it inside. Every stitch was a reminder to her of how awful she felt, every prick of the curved needle a reminder that she had cut herself because she'd been thinking about what a bad friend she was.

Maybe this is what I deserve, she told herself unhappily. *Maybe it will teach me not to do anything so stupid again.*

As Dr. Albion finished the last stitch and tied a knot in the thread, Annie saw someone enter the room. It was Eulalie. She walked over to the table and looked at the doctor as he worked.

"Now, why did you go trying to cut your finger clean off?" she asked Annie.

"I didn't do it on purpose," Annie replied. "I was cutting up carrots. For *your* dinner, I might add."

"Look at her," Eulalie said to Dr. Albion. "She's trying to blame this on *me*. Can you beat that?"

The doctor laughed as he wrapped gauze around Annie's stitched-up finger and secured it. "She'll be fine," he said. Then he looked at Annie. "Try not to bend your finger too much," he said. "It will heal faster if you don't. And come see me next week so we can see how this is doing."

Annie nodded. The doctor cleaned up the wrappers and other debris and left. When he was gone, Eulalie looked at Annie and frowned. "Still got that big old dog behind you, don't you?" she said.

"It was an *accident*," said Annie. "That's it."

Eulalie fixed her with a look that clearly implied that she wasn't buying it. "Who do you think you're talking to?" she asked. "I've been telling you for a week now that something is following you, and you keep telling me it ain't so. When are you going to stop trying to make me think everything is just fine?"

Annie looked down at the floor. She could feel the pain in her finger returning as the anesthesia wore off. It was like every beat of her heart sent a tiny stab of pain into her arm as the blood tried to push through her damaged skin. She looked up at Eulalie. "What is it you see?" she asked nervously.

Eulalie scanned the area around Annie, frowning. "Some kind of magic," she said. "Something powerful has got its arms wrapped around you but good."

"Magic?" said Annie. "You mean like a spell?"

"Something like," replied Eulalie. "But no simple spell, no. This is like something has been assigned to watch you."

Annie grew more and more nervous as Eulalie spoke. She didn't really understand what the old woman was saying, but it made her afraid.

"There's something tailing you, like I said," Eulalie informed her. "Looks to me like a big black dog that keeps getting bigger every time you turn around."

"Is it trying to hurt me?" asked Annie.

"No," replied Eulalie, shaking her head. "It wants you to do something, and it's pushing you to do it. That's why you cut your finger."

"This thing *made* me cut my finger?" Annie exclaimed. If it could do that, she thought, why couldn't it do something even worse?

"You did that yourself," said Eulalie. "But you

did it because you felt the breath of this spirit on your neck. It's standing close, child, no question about that."

"How do I get it to go away?" Annie asked.

Eulalie looked her in the eye. "You got to do what it wants," she said.

"But how do I know what that is?" Annie asked in frustration. "I don't even know who or what this thing is or how it got here."

"You might not know what it is," Eulalie said softly. "But I think you know what it wants."

Annie looked away from her. The old woman was right. Annie did know what was expected of her. She'd known for a long time. Despite what Becka had said, Annie knew that she had to somehow come clean about what she and Tyler had done—and what they'd almost done.

But why was this spirit pushing her to do it? How had it gotten to her? Those were questions that kept running through her mind. Did what she was experiencing have something to do with the Wiccan law of magic that stated that any energy someone sent out would come back to them three times as strong? Had what she and Tyler had done come back to haunt them, making their lives miserable because of their mistake? Or at least *her* life, anyway. She didn't know if Tyler was having any of the same problems.

"Can you help me make this thing stop following me?" Annie asked Eulalie.

"Might be I could," Eulalie answered. "But I'm not going to. Whatever this is about, this is about you. Me messing around in it doesn't help you any. You've got to face this thing all on your own."

Annie winced as renewed pain throbbed in her hand. She cupped her injured finger in her other hand and sat quietly for a minute, thinking. Had she really had her accident because the presence of something around her had made her lose concentration? Or had it just been an accident? She wanted to believe that it had just been an accident. But when she thought about it, she couldn't believe that. She'd been practicing the Craft for too long not to know that almost nothing happened for no reason. The cut had been a wake-up call to her.

Now she just had to decide how she was going to answer it.

CHAPTER 18

"What happened to your hand?" Cooper looked at the bandages around Annie's finger.

"Just some stitches," Annie told her, trying to sound casual.

"Is that why you weren't in school today?" Kate asked.

Annie nodded. "Aunt Sarah doesn't want me trying to carry stuff until this has had a chance to heal a little. But I'll be back pretty soon. Maybe Thursday if everything feels okay."

They were standing in the back room of Crones' Circle, waiting for their weekly class to begin. Only a few people had arrived already, so the room was quiet. The three of them stood there in an awkward silence.

"How did it happen?" asked Kate.

"A knife," said Annie. "I cut myself with a knife."

A knife, Kate thought. *Steel. Oggun likes knives.* Had Oggun really caused Annie to hurt herself? Was this the result of the ritual she'd done when she'd asked him for help? Looking at Annie's injured hand, she felt sick. Was she really responsible for her friend getting cut? And equally upsetting, did this prove her suspicions about Annie and Tyler? Either of those things being true would be enough to make her miserable. Both of them being true would be devastating.

You're the one who asked Oggun to punish her, she reminded herself. Then she wondered, if this had happened to Annie, had something happened to Tyler, too? Had he had some freak "accident" as well, caused by the orisha Kate had sent to take vengeance? Suddenly she realized what she'd done. She'd used magic against someone. And not just someone—her best friend and her boyfriend.

You were angry, she reminded herself. But she knew that was no excuse. Even if what she suspected was true, that was no reason for her to misuse magic.

"I forgot," she said suddenly. "There's something I need to go do."

"But what about class?" Cooper asked as Kate started to leave.

"I'll be back," Kate called out as she fled from the store.

She ran down the street as fast as she could. Her arms pumped as she forced her feet forward. Her chest began to burn as she breathed more and more heavily, but still she kept going. She blocked out the pain as she turned corners and looked for shortcuts.

Finally she reached Botanica Yemaya. She raced to the door and tried to open it, but it was locked. She looked at the sign on the door and saw that it had closed only a few minutes before. *Maybe someone is still there*, she thought.

She pounded on the door, praying that Evelyn or maybe Jon-Jon would still be somewhere in the back and hear her. She was frantic, and she felt her anxiety growing stronger and stronger as she stood, helpless, in front of the locked door peering into the dark store.

Then she saw movement in the darkness. Someone came to the door, and then she saw Madelaine's face looking out at her with a puzzled expression. When the girl saw that it was Kate outside, she undid the locks and pulled the door open.

"What's all the noise about?" she asked.

"Please," Kate said. "I need to talk to your mother. Is she here?"

"Yes," Madelaine said. "But what is this about?"

"Just let me in," Kate said. "Please. This is an emergency."

Madelaine stepped aside and motioned for Kate to come in. When she was inside the store, Madelaine locked the door again. "Come upstairs," she said.

Kate followed Madelaine through the doorway and then up a small staircase she had never noticed before. At the top of it Madelaine pushed open a door and led Kate inside. They were in an apartment, and Kate realized that Madelaine and her mother must live above the shop.

As they entered, Evelyn came out from another room. "Who was it?" she said, then noticed Kate standing there. The look on her face changed from one of curiosity to one of concern. "What's happened?" she asked.

"It's Annie," Kate said. "I mean, it's me, but what I did hurt Annie."

Evelyn frowned. "I don't understand," she said.

Kate looked at Madelaine, who was watching her with interest. She didn't really want the other girl to know what she'd done, but she was desperate. "I kind of did a ritual," Kate told Evelyn. "I asked Oggun to do something for me."

"What kind of something?" Evelyn asked, her voice low.

Kate swallowed. "I asked him to punish my boyfriend and the person I thought he was cheating on me with," she admitted.

Evelyn groaned. "And then your friend was hurt?" she said.

Kate nodded. "She cut herself with a knife. Not too badly, but she needed stitches."

Evelyn waved Kate to her. "Come," she said. "We need to talk."

Kate went to her, and Evelyn put an arm around her shoulder and led her into what turned out to be the kitchen. "Sit," she said, indicating a chair at the table.

Kate sat. She was a little disconcerted to see that Madelaine had followed them into the kitchen as well, but she didn't want to say anything about it. Madelaine leaned against the counter and listened as her mother talked.

"Orisha magic is very powerful," Evelyn told Kate. "You saw what the spirits do to people when they ride them."

Kate nodded. That was one of the things that had fascinated her most about the Santeria tradition.

Evelyn folded her hands on the table. "The orishas are not entirely like other spirits or gods," she said carefully. "They are not bad, or evil, but like humans they can become jealous and sometimes vengeful. It is possible to ask them to do what you did. There are people who do such things. However, this is not how you should interact with them. Oggun is your guardian spirit. He watches over you and protects you. When you asked him to do this thing, he became like an angry father. Do you understand?"

"I think so," Kate said. "He didn't like seeing me hurt, so he did as I asked and tried to make the people I thought hurt me pay for it."

Evelyn nodded. "Yes," she said. "Your anger fueled him. He was only doing as you asked."

"How do I stop him?" asked Kate.

"Probably it is done already," Evelyn told her.

"You asked to have the person your boyfriend was cheating on you with revealed, yes?"

"Yes," Kate said. "But what about the punishment part? I don't want anything to happen to Tyler."

"Then you must tell Papa Oggun that," Evelyn said.

"Can I do it now?" asked Kate.

Evelyn nodded. She got up and rummaged around the kitchen. "Maddy, hand me the bottle from the cupboard," she told her daughter as she herself looked in a drawer.

Madelaine did as her mother asked, and a moment later Evelyn placed some cigars, a bottle of rum, and a coconut on the table. "Take these to the park on the corner," she said. "Leave them under a tree. Give Oggun your thanks and tell him that he no longer needs to protect you from this."

Evelyn turned to Madelaine. "Go with her," she said. "Show her where to go."

Madelaine nodded. "Come on," she said to Kate.

Kate looked at Evelyn. "I'm really sorry," she said. "I didn't mean to do anything wrong. You were so nice to teach me about Santeria, and now I feel like I've ruined everything."

"You've ruined nothing that can't be fixed," Evelyn said, smiling. "We all fall down from time to time. The hard part is getting back up and moving on. You are always welcome in my store and in my home."

Kate took up the things on the table. "Thank you," she said to Evelyn, and then followed Madelaine out of the apartment and down the stairs.

"There is a tree in this park that is used by many people in the religion," Madelaine explained as they walked to the corner. "It is considered sacred."

Kate nodded. She felt strange being alone with Madelaine. It bothered her that the girl knew what she had done. *What must she think of me?* Kate wondered as they entered the park.

Madelaine led her to a remote corner of the park, away from the benches and the fountain. There she stopped in front of a large tree. "This is it," she said, a note of reverence in her voice. "You may make your offering here. I will wait for you."

Kate nodded and Madelaine left her alone. Kate knelt. Looking at the base of the tree, she was surprised to see that objects of various kinds were already scattered around it. Flowers, candies, nails, and pieces of paper with writing on them covered the roots. Kate wondered what the people who had come before her had asked of the orishas. Had any of them, like her, made mistakes that they needed to make up for?

She couldn't think about that now. She cleared her head and thought about what she needed to do. She nestled the cigars and the coconut in a little nook made by the tree's roots. Then she opened the bottle of rum and poured it over the ground around the tree. The sweet smell filled her nose and made her choke a little bit.

"Oggun," she said when she had emptied the bottle. "Thank you for listening to me, and for coming to my protection. But now please don't do any more. I was wrong in asking for you to do those things, and I'm sorry for that. I know you were only looking out for one of your children."

She didn't know what else to say. What she had said was hard enough to get out. Part of her was afraid that Oggun would be angry at her for asking him to do something she really hadn't wanted him to do. But she really *was* sorry, and she hoped that was enough.

After sitting there for another minute, Kate got up and looked around for Madelaine. She saw her standing beneath a street lamp not too far away. Walking over to her, she said, "Thanks for showing me where to go."

Madelaine smiled at her. "Mama was right," she said. "We've all done things like what you did."

"Really?" Kate asked doubtfully. "You mean I'm not the only stupid one?"

Madelaine laughed. "No," she said. "I've seen people do *much* stupider things. Someday I'll tell you about the ones *I've* done."

"That makes me feel a little better, I guess," Kate said. "But this isn't over yet. I still have something else to do."

Madelaine nodded. "Go," she said.

Kate paused. "Thanks," she said. "I know we don't

really know each other very well, but I hope we get to."

"I think that can be arranged," Madelaine told her. "Just tell your friend that I'm not after her boyfriend. If she's anything like you, I'd be in big trouble."

Kate laughed. "I'll do that," she said.

She left Madelaine at the entrance to the park and started running again. This time she went a little more slowly. She needed to think about exactly what she was going to do. By the time she reached Crones' Circle, she was ready. Or at least she hoped she was.

She went inside. Class was just ending and people were helping to put away the chairs and the other items they'd used during the session. Kate looked around and saw Annie and Cooper standing to one side. They were talking to Tyler.

Here goes nothing, Kate told herself, and walked over to them.

"Hi," she said.

The three of them looked at her.

"Hi," Cooper said. "Are you okay? You look beat."

"I'm okay," Kate said. "I was running." Then she turned to Annie and Tyler. "We need to talk," she said.

Tyler and Annie exchanged a look. "Yeah," Tyler said. "We do."

"But not here," said Kate. "How about on the beach?"

Tyler nodded. "Okay," he said.

"That's fine," added Annie, looking very sad.

"I think I'll just go," Cooper said. "I'll talk to you guys later, okay?"

Kate and the others nodded. Cooper left, and the three of them exited the store behind her and walked toward the wharf, not saying anything. They continued in silence down the long flight of wooden stairs to the beach. Then they walked along the shore.

"It seems like all kinds of important stuff happens to me down here," Kate remarked as they walked. "I broke up with Scott here. I first kissed you here," she said, looking at Tyler. "I did my first ritual with you here," she added, glancing at Annie. "It's like the ocean sees all these major things in my life."

"Kate . . ." Tyler said.

"No," Kate said. "Let me finish. I know something happened between the two of you. I don't know what, exactly, but I know it changed things. And I know that thinking about it made me so angry that I did something I would never think I could do—I hurt one of my best friends in the whole world. Annie, I'm sorry about your accident."

"You didn't—" Annie began.

"Yes, I did," said Kate. "I'll tell you how later. The point is that I did it and I'm sorry."

"And I'm sorry for not telling you everything," Annie said.

Kate held up her hand. "You know what," she said. "I don't really even want to know. But I do want to know where it leaves us," she said to Tyler.

Tyler looked at her, his eyes glinting in the moonlight. "I think we should probably stop seeing each other," he said. "There's nothing between Annie and me. Something happened, and it happened for a lot of reasons. It wasn't right, but it made me see that this isn't working for you and me right now, Kate."

Kate felt something inside of her break. Not her heart, but a dam that had been holding back a lot of emotions. Now she was surprised to see that although she mostly felt sad, she also felt a sense of relief. It was as if a huge source of pressure had been taken off her. She didn't entirely understand why, but she felt better.

"Okay," she said simply.

No one spoke for a few minutes as they stood on the beach, the waves crashing in and the cold November wind blowing across their faces. Above them, the moon was bright and sharp, and the stars shone like bits of cut glass in the sky.

"I don't know what else to say," Tyler said finally.

"You don't have to say anything," Kate said. "We can talk more about it later. Right now I think we should just call it a night."

They walked back up the steps. At the top, Tyler

paused. "This feels weird," he said. "I don't know what to do now."

"Go home," Kate told him. "That's what I'm going to do."

"Okay," Tyler said. "I guess I'll just say good-night, then."

He turned and left Kate standing with Annie. When he was gone, Annie said, "I understand if you don't want to be my friend anymore."

Kate looked at her. Annie's hands were pushed into the pockets of her coat, and she was shivering in the cold. Her hair was blowing around, and from time to time she pushed it out of her face before plunging her hand back into her pocket. Every time she did Kate looked at the white bandage wrapped around her finger.

"I'm really mad at you right now," Kate said. "Really mad."

Annie nodded. "I'm mad at me, too, if that helps any."

"It doesn't," Kate said. "I just need to be mad."

Annie looked away.

"But I won't be mad forever," Kate told her, and Annie looked back at her. Her eyes were wet.

"You're my best friend, Kate," she said. "If I could take this back, I would. But I can't."

Kate shook her head. "We shouldn't talk about this right now," she said. "I need some time to cool off. I just wanted to tell you that I'm sorry about your hand and that I still really love you."

"I love you, too, Kate," Annie whispered.

Kate breathed deeply. "I think I need to be alone now, if that's okay."

Annie nodded. "We'll talk later?" she asked.

"Yeah," Kate said. "We will."

Annie gave her friend one last long look and then turned and walked in the direction of the bus stop. Kate watched her for a minute and then turned around. Leaning against the railing of the wharf, she stared out at the ocean. And she began to cry. But even as the tears fell, she knew that, inside, she was beginning to heal. It would just take time. How much time, she didn't know. But she knew that she would, and she knew that when it was over she would be stronger than she'd ever been.

She sniffed the air. Suddenly she smelled smoke. Cigar smoke. Turning around, she looked to see if someone was walking along behind her. But there was no one there. Still, the smell was growing stronger. It surrounded her.

She reached into her coat and touched the string of green and black beads she was wearing beneath her shirt. "I'm glad you liked the presents," she said, and started walking home.

follow the

circle of three

with book 11:
The House of winter

"Is that it?" Kate asked, her voice filled with awe.

"That's it," confirmed Sophia.

"Wow," Cooper said simply.

"Double wow," echoed Annie.

Before them sat a huge, old hotel. It was situated in the center of a ring of snowy mountains, the tops of which rose up around it. The hotel itself was enormous, an elaborate Victorian building with ornate carvings, several tower rooms with pointed roofs, and stained-glass windows looking out at them like multicolored eyes. Two wings of rooms stretched out on either side of the main building, and smoke puffed gently from several chimneys.

"It's beautiful," Annie said as Sophia pulled the SUV up to the front and parked it beside some other cars that were already there.

"Wait until you see the inside," said Sophia. "Come on."

They got out and retrieved their bags from the

back of the car. Then they walked up the neatly shoveled path to the front steps of the hotel and went through the door. Once inside, the girls set down their bags and looked around in awe.

The lobby of the hotel was done in red. Almost everything was red, from the deep red of the walls to the red velvet upholstery on the couches and chairs that were arranged in comfortable groups all around the enormous room. A huge chandelier, its hundreds of individual crystals sparkling with light, hung from the ceiling over their heads, and classical music floated softly through the air.

"Look at that tree," Annie said, nodding at an enormous pine tree that stood in the center of the lobby. Its spreading branches were strung with what seemed to be thousands of white lights, and ornaments of all kinds hung from it.

"That's the Yule tree," Sophia told them. "The ornaments on it have been used since the hotel opened. Every year they add some new ones, but some of those are almost a hundred and fifty years old."

"Sophia!"

A woman emerged from a doorway behind the long wooden check-in counter, distracting them from looking at the tree. She had deep red hair that complemented the colors of the lobby, and she was wearing a burgundy-colored shirt with jeans. She walked quickly toward them and embraced Sophia warmly.

"Fiona," Sophia said. "Merry meet."

Fiona laughed as she released her friend from the hug. "Merry meet yourself," she replied gaily. "It's been a long time."

"Since last Yule," Sophia said. "How are Bryan and the girls?"

"See for yourself," answered Fiona. Then she turned and called out, "Sophia's here," in a loud voice.

Moments later a man emerged from the doorway. A little shorter than his wife, he had curly black hair and an easy, crooked smile that made his chin dimple. He, too, came over and hugged Sophia.

"Has it really been a whole year?" he asked, shaking his head. "It seems like you were just here."

"It goes by quickly," Sophia told him. "I bet the girls are all grown up now."

"They'll be sixteen this Yule," Bryan said.

"Where are they, honey?" Fiona asked her husband.

"They could be anywhere," he answered. "I'm sure they'll turn up."

"I wanted them to meet *my* girls," Sophia said. "Bryan and Fiona, this is Cooper, Kate, and Annie. They're part of my group this year."

Fiona and Bryan shook hands with the three girls. "You willingly signed up for her boot camp?" Bryan asked them, cocking his head at Sophia. "You're braver than I am."

"She's not so bad once you get the drill down," Cooper deadpanned.

Bryan laughed as Sophia pretended to be horrified by Cooper's remark. Then the front door opened and another group of people came in.

"Bryan, why don't you take this bunch up to their rooms while I say hello to the new arrivals," Fiona said.

"Will do," answered Bryan. "Follow me, folks," he added to Kate, Annie, Cooper, and Sophia.

They picked up their bags and followed as Bryan walked down the hallway that stretched to the left away from the lobby. The corridor seemed to go on forever, then they came to a staircase and Bryan started up it.

"We saved you the best rooms in the house," he remarked as they climbed.

"Ah," Sophia said. "The ghost rooms."

"That would be them," Bryan replied.

"Ghost rooms?" Annie asked.

"Indeed," Bryan told her. "Didn't Sophia tell you that the hotel is haunted?"

"By who?" Cooper said.

"All kinds of people," said Bryan as they ascended another flight of stairs. "Doomed lovers. Murdered gangsters. Failed businessmen. All kinds of people died in this place."

"How cheery," remarked Kate grimly as she switched her bag to her other shoulder. "So, which ones do we get?"

Bryan went up a final set of stairs, and they

found themselves in another hallway. "You get the best ones of all," he told them as they walked halfway down and stopped in front of a door. Bryan took out a key and held it up. "You get the honeymoon ghosts."

The girls looked at each other. "Okay," Cooper said, "I'll bite. What's the story?"

Bryan grinned wickedly. "It's quite a story," he replied. "It happened in 1923. A young couple, Rose and Edgar Whiting, came to the hotel to get married and to spend their honeymoon here. It was a grand affair. They rented the entire place. The rooms were filled with their guests. On the day they married, Rose was beautiful in her wedding dress and Edgar was as handsome as could be in his tuxedo. The wedding party afterward was legendary, lasting long into the night. Finally, in the early hours of the morning, the couple retired to these rooms."

Bryan paused dramatically, letting them all wonder what could possibly come next. After an agonizing wait, he continued. "When the maid came in the morning to bring Rose and Edgar their breakfasts, she found them . . . dead."

"Dead how?" Annie asked.

"Aren't you a morbid one?" commented Bryan, looking at Annie curiously.

"It's not a good story unless we know the how part," Cooper explained.

"This is quite a bunch you have here," Bryan

said to Sophia. Then he turned back to the girls. "That's the strange part," he said. "Rose had been poisoned and Edgar had been shot through the heart. But no one could tell which of them had died first, so they never knew if it was murder or some kind of suicide pact."

"Why would they kill themselves on their wedding night?" Kate said. "That doesn't make sense. Of course, they had to have been murdered."

"That's what the police thought," Bryan said. "Except that the door was locked from the inside. The maid had to use her key to open it."

"But if she had a key, someone else could have had one as well, right?" said Cooper skeptically.

"There were only two of them," Bryan said. "This is one of them." He waved the key in his hand at them. "The other one is in the hotel office."

"A locked-door mystery," Annie said. "How very Agatha Christie."

"And this one was never solved," Bryan said. "To this day no one knows what happened in these rooms. But people who have stayed here report that all kinds of weird things happen."

"What kinds of things?" Cooper asked.

"Voices," Bryan answered. "Glimpses of shadowy figures. Things disappearing. Faces in the mirrors. Think you can handle it?"

Cooper laughed, and Bryan looked surprised. "I grew up with a ghost," Cooper informed him. "And let's just say that all three of us have friends in the spirit world."

Bryan cocked an eyebrow. "Then this should prove to be very interesting," he said as he inserted the key in the lock and turned it.